KT-449-574

FIFE EDUCATION COMMITTEE
ST. COLUMBA'S
SCHOOL
DUNFERMLINE

17

SHORT STORIES

READING TODAY

The Purple Plain	H. E. BATES
Sammy Going South	W. H. CANAWAY
The Happy Return	C. S. FORESTER
From Merciless Invaders	ALEXANDER McKEE
Thrush Green	'MISS READ'
Nautilus 90 North	COMMANDER ANDERSON AND CLAY BLAIR JR.
Spy Catcher	ORESTE PINTO
Mystery and Suspense	Ed: ARTHUR J. ARKLEY
Short Stories	Ed: S. D. KNEEBONE
Niki: The Story of a Dog	TIBOR DERY
The Franchise Affair	JOSEPHINE TEY
Jamaica Inn	DAPHNE DU MAURIER

COMPILED AND EDITED BY
S. D. KNEEBONE

Short Stories

NELSON

THOMAS NELSON AND SONS LTD

36 Park Street London W1
P.O. Box 336 Apapa Lagos
P.O. Box 25012 Nairobi
P.O. Box 21149 Dar es Salaam
P.O. Box 2187 Accra
77 Coffee Street San Fernando Trinidad

THOMAS NELSON (AUSTRALIA) LTD
597 Little Collins Street Melbourne 3000

THOMAS NELSON AND SONS (SOUTH AFRICA) (PROPRIETARY) LTD
51 Commissioner Street Johannesburg

THOMAS NELSON AND SONS (CANADA) LTD
81 Curlew Drive Don Mills Ontario

THOMAS NELSON AND SONS
Copewood and Davis Streets Camden New Jersey 08103

———

First edition 1965
© *Thomas Nelson and Sons Ltd 1965*
Reprinted 1969

17 443507 X

COVER ILLUSTRATION BY QUENTIN BLAKE

Printed in Great Britain by Butler & Tanner Ltd, Frome and London

CONTENTS

ACKNOWLEDGMENTS

For permission to reprint copyright stories grateful thanks are due to the trustees of the estate of James Thurber and Hamish Hamilton Ltd for 'The White Rabbit Caper' from *Vintage Thurber Vol I*, The Bodley Head Ltd for 'The Open Window' from *The Bodley Head Saki*, Liam O'Flaherty and Jonathan Cape Ltd for 'The Reapers' from *The Tent*, William Sansom and The Hogarth Press Ltd for 'The Vertical Ladder' from *Something Terrible, Something Lovely*, Giovanni Guareschi, Victor Gollancz Ltd and Farrar Straus & Co Inc for 'A Confession' and 'The Defeat' from *The Little World of Don Camillo*, Frank O'Connor and Hamish Hamilton Ltd for 'The Miser' from *Domestic Relations*, Evelyn Waugh for 'Tactical Exercise', Phyllis Bottome and Faber and Faber Ltd for 'Henry' from *Man and Beast*, the executors of the estate of Dorothy L. Sayers and Victor Gollancz Ltd for 'The Man Who Knew How' from *A Treasury of Sayers Stories*, Daphne du Maurier and Victor Gollancz Ltd for 'The Old Man' from *The Apple Tree*, John Wyndham and Michael Joseph Ltd for 'Compassion Circuit' from *The Seeds of Time*, H. E. Bates and Michael Joseph Ltd for 'The Diamond Hair-pin' from *The Fabulous Mrs V*, L. P. Hartley and Hamish Hamilton Ltd for 'A High Dive' from *Two For The River*, Doris Lessing and MacGibbon and Kee Ltd for 'Through the Tunnel' from *The Habit of Loving*, Isaac Asimov, Dennis Dobson and Doubleday & Co Inc for 'The Feeling of Power' from *Nine Tomorrows*.

PREFACE

SHORT stories are one of the most attractive forms of literature. Like the novel, they have descended from the fables and epics of the past.

Somewhere in the dim recesses of history, the first short story was told. Perhaps the teller was a caveman, huddled with his family around their protective fire. Through succeeding ages, story-tellers have captured and enthralled their audiences with an almost infinite variety of stories in every known tongue.

Perhaps one of the greatest story-tellers of all time was Jesus Christ of Nazareth. Such stories as 'The Good Samaritan' and 'The Prodigal Son', which he used to illustrate his teachings, are among the best the world has known.

During the Middle Ages professional story-tellers arose, the minstrels and the bards who put their stories into verse and sang them to the accompaniment of the harp or lyre. Unsophisticated as these stories may seem, they had a charm and simplicity which beguiled the tedium of weary hours. Such are the Canterbury Tales by Chaucer—stories told by pilgrims to enliven their journey from Southwark to the shrine of St. Thomas. Story-telling then was an art which flourished.

During the eighteenth and nineteenth centuries it entered a decline, but today it is happily regaining its earlier robust health and vigour. This new appeal is no doubt due in part to the speed of modern life, when people are unable to accept the more spacious and leisurely treatment of Victorian times. The demand is for something short and snappy. Television, too, has helped by providing the ideal medium for the short story writer.

The art of writing a short story is a difficult one. First of all a short story should be true to its name, it should be a story, and it should be short. One of the most effective ghost stories ever was told in one sentence: 'So you don't believe in ghosts?' said the stranger in the railway carriage, and vanished.

Even shorter is the sad tale of Algy.

> Algy met a bear,
> The bear was bulgy,
> The bulge was Algy.

Of course no one would suggest that brevity always be carried to these extremes.

The modern short story is very difficult to define. It may have any subject under the sun; it may be tough or gentle, powerful or fragile, passionate or restrained. What it must possess above all else is that subtle, elusive, indefinable power which invests a story with reality.

In this respect the writers of these stories are craftsmen of the highest order. I can only hope that you will gain from them as much pleasure and enjoyment as I have done.

S. D. K.

James Thurber

JAMES THURBER was born in America, at Columbus, Ohio. For the first seven years of his life he was very sickly and unable to keep anything in his stomach. Despite this he grew to six feet one and a half inches tall, and weighed, so he said, one hundred and fifty-four pounds fully dressed for winter.

He began to write when he was ten years old, and to draw when he was fourteen. He became equally famous as a writer and as a cartoonist.

His memory was amazing. He could rattle off the names, phone numbers, and birthdays of every one of his friends, and even the birthdays of all their children.

He settled down in Connecticut where he spent his retirement reading *Huckleberry Finn*, raising poodles, and laying down a wine-cellar.

Thurber's writing is refreshing and original. He himself confessed that his prose pieces start at the beginning and seem to reach the middle by way of the end.

THE WHITE RABBIT CAPER

FRED FOX was pouring himself a slug of rye when the door of his office opened and in hopped old Mrs. Rabbit. She was a white rabbit with pink eyes, and she wore a shawl on her head, and gold-rimmed spectacles.

'I want you to find Daphne,' she said tearfully, and she handed Fred Fox a snapshot of a rabbit with pink eyes that looked to him like a picture of every other white rabbit with pink eyes.

'When did she hop the hutch?' asked Fred Fox.

'Yesterday,' said old Mrs. Rabbit. 'She is only eighteen

1

months old, and I am afraid that some superstitious creature has killed her for one of her feet.'

Fred Fox turned the snapshot over and put it in his pocket. 'Has this bunny got a throb?' he asked.

'Yes,' said old Mrs. Rabbit. 'Franz Frog, repulsive owner of the notorious Lily Pad Night Club.'

Fred Fox leaped to his feet. 'Come on, Grandma,' he said, 'and don't step on your ears. We got to move fast.'

On the way to the Lily Pad Night Club, old Mrs. Rabbit scampered so fast that Fred Fox had all he could do to keep up with her. 'Daphne is my great-great-great-great-great-grand-daughter, if my memory serves,' said old Mrs. Rabbit. 'I have thirty-nine thousand descendants.'

'This isn't going to be easy,' said Fred Fox. ' Maybe you should have gone to a magician with a hat.'

'But she is the only one named Daphne,' said old Mrs. Rabbit, 'and she lived alone with me on my great carrot farm.'

They came to a broad brook. 'Skip it!' asked Fred Fox.

'Keep a civil tongue in your head, young man,' snapped old Mrs. Rabbit.

Just as they got to the Lily Pad, a dandelion clock struck twelve noon. Fred Fox pushed the button on the great green door, on which was painted a white water lily. The door opened an eighth of an inch, and Ben Rat peered out. 'Beat it,' he said, but Fred Fox shoved the door open, and old Mrs. Rabbit followed him into a cool green hallway, softly but restlessly lighted by thousands of fireflies imprisoned in the hollow crystal pendants of an enormous chandelier. At the right there was a flight of green-carpeted stairs, and at the bottom of the steps the door to the cloakroom. Straight ahead, at the end of the long hallway, was the cool green door to Franz Frog's office.

'Beat it,' said Ben Rat again.

'Talk nice,' said Fred Fox, 'or I'll seal your house up with tin. Where's the Croaker?'

'Once a gumpaw, always a gumpaw,' grumbled Ben Rat. 'He's in his office.'

'With Daphne?'

'Who's Daphne?' asked Ben Rat.

'My great-great-great-great-great-granddaughter,' said old Mrs. Rabbit.

'Nobody's that great,' snarled Ben Rat.

Fred Fox opened the cool green door and went into Franz Frog's office, followed by old Mrs. Rabbit and Ben Rat. The owner of the Lily Pad sat behind his desk, wearing a green suit, green shirt, green tie, green socks, and green shoes. He had an emerald tiepin and seven emerald rings. 'Whong you wong, Fonnxx?' he rumbled in a cold, green, cavernous voice. His eyes bulged and his throat began to swell ominously.

'He's going to croak,' explained Ben Rat.

'Nuts,' said Fred Fox. 'He'll outlive all of us.'

'Glunk,' croaked Franz Frog.

Ben Rat glared at Fred Fox. 'You oughta go on the stage,' he snarled.

'Where's Daphne?' demanded Fred Fox.

'Hoong Dangneng?' asked Franz Frog.

'Your Bunny friend,' said Fred Fox.

'Nawng,' said Franz Frog.

Fred Fox picked up a cello in a corner and put it down. It was too light to contain a rabbit. The front door-bell rang. 'I'll get it,' said Fred Fox. It was Oliver (Hoot) Owl, a notorious fly-by-night. 'What're you doing up at this hour, Hoot?' asked Fred Fox.

'I'm trying to blind myself, so I'll confess,' said Hoot Owl testily.

'Confess to what?' snapped Fred Fox.

'What can't you solve?' asked Hoot Owl.

'The disappearance of Daphne,' said Fred Fox.

'Who's Daphne?' asked Hoot Owl.

Franz Frog hopped out of his office into the hall. Ben Rat and old Mrs. Rabbit followed him.

Down the steps from the second floor came Sherman Stork, carrying a white muffler or something and grinning foolishly.

'Well, bless my soul!' said Fred Fox. 'If it isn't old mid-husband himself! What did you do with Daphne?'

'Who's Daphne?' asked Sherman Stork.

'Fox thinks somebody killed Daphne Rabbit,' said Ben Rat.

'Fonnxx cung brong,' rumbled Franz Frog.

'I *could* be wrong,' said Fred Fox, 'but I'm not.' He pulled open the cloakroom door at the bottom of the steps, and the dead body of a female white rabbit toppled furrily on to the cool green carpet. Her head had been bashed in by a heavy blunt instrument.

'Daphne!' screamed old Mrs. Rabbit, bursting into tears.

'I can't see a thing,' said Hoot Owl.

'It's a dead white rabbit,' said Ben Rat. 'Anybody can see that. You're dumb.'

'I'm wise!'' said Hoot Owl indignantly. 'I know everything.'

'Jeeng Crine,' moaned Franz Frog. He stared up at the chandelier, his eyes bulging and his mammoth mouth gaping open. All the fireflies were frightened and went out.

The cool green hallway became pitch black. There was a shriek in the dark, and a feathery 'plump'. The fireflies lighted up to see what had happened. Hoot Owl lay dead on the cool green carpet, his head bashed in by a heavy blunt instrument. Ben Rat, Franz Frog, Sherman Stork, old Mrs. Rabbit, and Fred Fox stared at Hoot Owl. He lay like a feather duster.

'Murder!' squealed old Mrs. Rabbit.

'Nobody leaves this hallway!' snapped Fred Fox. 'There's a killer loose in this club!'

'I am not used to death,' said Sherman Stork.

'Roong!' groaned Franz Frog.

'He says he's ruined,' said Ben Rat, but Fred Fox wasn't listening. He was looking for a heavy blunt instrument. There wasn't any.

'Search them!' cried old Mrs. Rabbit. 'Somebody has a sap, or a sock full of sand, or something!'

'Yeh,' said Fred Fox. 'Ben Rat is a sap—maybe someone swung him by his tail.'

'You oughta go on the stage,' snarled Ben Rat.

Fred Fox searched the suspects, but he found no concealed weapon. 'You could have strangled them with that muffler,' Fred Fox told Sherman Stork.

'But they were not strangled,' said Sherman Stork.

Fred Fox turned to Ben Rat. 'You could have bitten them to death with your ugly teeth,' he said.

'But they weren't bitten to death,' said Ben Rat.

Fred Fox stared at Franz Frog. 'You could have scared them to death with your ugly face,' he said.

'Bung wung screng ta deng,' said Franz Frog.

'You're right,' admitted Fred Fox. 'They weren't. Where's old Mrs. Rabbit?' he asked suddenly.

'I'm hiding in here,' called old Mrs. Rabbit from the cloakroom. 'I'm frightened.'

Fred Fox got her out of the cool green sanctuary and went in himself. It was dark. He groped around on the cool green carpet. He didn't know what he was looking for, but he found it, a small object lying in a far corner. He put it in his pocket and came out of the cloakroom.

'What'd you find, shamus?' asked Ben Rat apprehensively.

'Exhibit A,' said Fred Fox casually.

'Sahng plang keeng,' moaned Franz Frog.

'He says somebody's playing for keeps,' said Ben Rat.

'He can say that again,' said Fred Fox as the front door was flung open and Inspector Mastiff trotted in, followed by Sergeant Dachshund.

'Well, well, look who's muzzling in,' said Fred Fox.

'What have we got here?' barked Inspector Mastiff.

'I hate a private nose,' said Sergeant Dachshund.

Fred Fox grinned at him. 'What happened to your legs from the knees down, sport?' he asked.

'Drop dead,' snarled Sergeant Dachshund.

'Quiet, both of you!' snapped Inspector Mastiff. 'I know Ollie Owl, but who's the twenty dollar Easter present from Schrafft's?' He turned on Fred Fox. 'If this bunny's head comes off and she's filled with candy, I'll have your badge, Fox,' he growled.

'She's real, Inspector,' said Fred Fox. 'Real dead, too. How did you pick up the scent?'

Inspector Mastiff howled. 'The sergeant thought he smelt a rat at the Lily Club,' he said. 'Wrong again, as usual. Who's this dead rabbit?'

She's my great-great-great-great-great-granddaughter,' sobbed old Mrs. Rabbit.

Fred Fox lighted a cigarette. 'Oh no, she isn't, sweetheart,' he said coolly. 'You are her great-great-great-great-great-granddaughter.' Pink lightning flared in the live white rabbit's eyes. 'You killed the old lady, so you could take over her carrot farm,' continued Fred Fox, 'and then you killed Hoot Owl.'

'I'll kill you too, shamus!' shrieked Daphne Rabbit.

'Put the cuffs on her, sergeant,' barked Inspector Mastiff. Sergeant Dachshund put a pair of handcuffs on the front legs of the dead rabbit. 'Not her, you dumb kraut!' yelped Inspector Mastiff. It was too late. Daphne Rabbit had jumped through a window pane and run away, with the Sergeant in hot pursuit.

'All white rabbits look alike to me,' growled Inspector Mastiff. 'How could you tell them apart—from their ears?'

'No,' said Fred Fox. 'From their years. The white rabbit that called on me darn near beat me to the Lily Pad, and no old woman can do that.'

'Don't brag,' said Inspector Mastiff. 'Spryness isn't enough. What else?'

'She understood expressions an old rabbit doesn't know,' said Fred Fox, 'like "hop the hutch" and "throb" and "skip it" and "sap".'

'You can't hang a rabbit for her vocabulary,' said Inspector Mastiff. 'Come again.'

Fred Fox pulled the snapshot out of his pocket. 'The white rabbit who called on me told me Daphne was eighteen months old,' he said, 'but read what it says on the back of this picture.'

Inspector Mastiff took the snapshot, turned it over, and read, 'Daphne on her second birthday.'

'Yes,' said Fred Fox. 'Daphne knocked six months off her age. 'You see, Inspector, she couldn't read the writing on the snapshot, because those weren't her spectacles she was wearing.'

'Now wait a minute,' growled Inspector Mastiff. 'Why did she kill Hoot Owl?'

'Elementary, my dear Mastiff,' said Fred Fox. 'Hoot Owl lived in an oak tree, and she was afraid he saw her burrowing into the club last night, dragging Grandma. She heard Hoot Owl say, 'I'm wise. I know everything,' and so she killed him.'

'What with?' demanded the Inspector.

'Her right hind foot,' said Fred Fox. 'I was looking for a concealed weapon, and all the time she was carrying her heavy blunt instrument openly.'

'Well, what do you know!' exclaimed Inspector Mastiff. 'Do you think Hoot Owl really saw her?'

'Could be,' said Fred Fox. 'I happen to think he was bragging about his wisdom in general and not about a particular piece of information, but your guess is as good as mine.'

'What did you pick up in the cloakroom?' squeaked Ben Rat.

'The final strand of rope that will hang Daphne,' said Fred Fox. 'I knew she didn't go in there to hide. She went in there to look for something she lost last night. If she'd been frightened she would have hidden when the flies went out, but she went in there after the flies lighted up again.'

'That adds up,' said Inspector Mastiff grudgingly. 'What was it she was looking for?'

'Well,' said Fred Fox, 'she heard something drop in the dark when she dragged Grandma in there last night and she thought it was a button, or a buckle, or a bead, or a bangle, or a brooch that would incriminate her. That's why she rang me in on the case. She couldn't come here alone to look for it.'

'Well, what was it, Fox?' snapped Inspector Mastiff.

'A carrot,' said Fred Fox, and he took it out of his pocket, 'probably fell out of old Mrs. Rabbit's reticule, if you like irony.'

'One more question,' said Inspector Mastiff. 'Why plant the body in the Lily Pad?'

'Easy,' said Fred Fox. 'She wanted to throw suspicion on the Croaker, a well-known lady-killer.'

'Nawng,' rumbled Franz Frog.

'Well, there it is, Inspector,' said Fred Fox, 'all wrapped up for you and tied with ribbon.'

Ben Rat disappeared into a wall. Franz Frog hopped back to his office.

'Mercy!' cried Sherman Stork. 'I'm late for an appointment!' He flew to the front door and opened it.

There stood Daphne Rabbit, holding the unconscious form of Sergeant Dachshund. 'I give up,' she said, 'I surrender.'

'Is he dead?' asked Inspector Mastiff hopefully.

'No,' said Daphne Rabbit. 'He fainted.'

'I never have any luck,' growled Inspector Mastiff.

Fred Fox leaned over and pointed to Daphne's right hind leg. 'Owl feathers,' he said. 'She's all yours, Inspector.'

'Thanks, Fox,' said Inspector Mastiff. 'I'll throw something your way someday.'

'Make it a nice, plump Plymouth Rock pullet,' said Fred Fox, and he sauntered out of the Lily Pad.

Back in his office, Fred Fox dictated his report on the White Rabbit Caper to his secretary, Lura Fox. 'Period. End of report,' he said finally, toying with an emerald stick-pin he had taken from Franz Frog's green necktie when the fireflies went out.

'Is she pretty?' asked Lura Fox.

'Daphne? Quite a dish,' said Fred Fox, 'But I like my rabbits stewed, and I'm afraid little Daphne is going to fry.'

'But she's so young, Fred!' cried Lura Fox. 'Only eighteen months!'

'You weren't listening,' said Fred Fox.

'How did you know she wasn't interested in Franz Frog?' asked Lura Fox.

'Simple,' said Fred Fox. 'Wrong species.'

'What became of the candy, Fred?' asked Lura Fox.

Fred Fox stared at her. 'What candy?' he asked blankly.

Lura Fox suddenly burst into tears. 'She was so soft, and warm, and cuddly, Fred,' she wailed.

Fred Fox filled a glass with rye, drank it slowly, set down the glass, and sighed grimly, 'Sour racket,' he said.

From *Vintage Thurber Vol. I* by James Thurber,
Copyright © 1963, Hamish Hamilton, London.

Hector Hugh Munro

HECTOR HUGH MUNRO was born in Burma and educated at Bedford School. His childhood was not altogether happy. It was during those years that he was hauled by his father round half of Europe.

When he was old enough, he joined the Burma Mounted Police, but was forced to resign through ill health. He returned to England, became a journalist, and wrote stories under the pseudonym 'Saki'— the name of the cup-bearer in Omar Khayyam's *Rubaiyat*.

Although he was over age, Munro enlisted in the First World War as a trooper in King Edward's Horse. He was twice offered a commission, but refused, and in 1916 he was killed in action.

Saki's stories are unique, sparkling with wit and razor-sharp thrusts. He springs surprises at most unexpected moments, and with the most urbane manner in the world.

THE OPEN WINDOW

'MY AUNT will be down presently, Mr. Nuttel,' said a very self-possessed young lady of fifteen; 'in the meantime you must try and put up with me.'

Framton Nuttel endeavoured to say the correct something which should duly flatter the niece of the moment without unduly discounting the aunt that was to come. Privately he doubted more than ever whether these formal visits on a succession of total strangers would do much towards helping the nerve cure which he was supposed to be undergoing.

'I know how it will be,' his sister had said when he was preparing to migrate to this rural retreat; 'you will bury yourself down there and not speak to a living soul, and your nerves will be worse than ever from moping. I shall just give you letters of introduction to all the people I know there. Some of them, as far as I can remember, were quite nice.'

Framton wondered whether Mrs. Sappleton, the lady to whom he was presenting one of the letters of introduction, came into the nice division.

'Do you know many of the people round here?' asked the niece, when she judged that they had had sufficient silent communion.

'Hardly a soul,' said Framton. ' My sister was staying here, at the rectory, you know, some four years ago, and she gave me letters of introduction to some of the people here.'

He made the last statement in a tone of distinct regret.

'Then you know practically nothing about my aunt?' pursued the self-possessed young lady.

'Only her name and address,' admitted the caller. He was wondering whether Mrs. Sappleton was in the married or widowed state. An undefinable something about the room seemed to suggest masculine habitation.

'Her great tragedy happened just three years ago,' said the child; 'that would be since your sister's time.'

'Her tragedy?' asked Framton; somehow in this restful country spot tragedies seemed out of place.

'You may wonder why we keep that window wide open on an October afternoon,' said the niece, indicating a large French window that opened on the lawn.

'It is quite warm for the time of the year,' said Framton; 'but has that window got anything to do with the tragedy?'

'Out through that window, three years ago to a day, her husband and her two young brothers went off to their day's shooting. They never came back. In crossing the moor to their favourite snipe-shooting ground they were all three engulfed in a treacherous piece of bog. It had been that dreadful wet summer, you know, and places that were safe in other years gave way suddenly without warning. Their bodies were never recovered. That was the dreadful part of it.' Here the child's voice lost its self-possessed note and became falteringly human. 'Poor aunt always thinks that they will come back some day, they and the little brown spaniel that was lost with them, and walk in at that window just as they used to do. That is why the window is kept open every evening till it is quite dusk. Poor dear aunt, she has often told me how they went out, her husband with his white waterproof coat over his arm, and Ronnie, her youngest brother, singing 'Bertie, why do you bound?' as he always did to tease her, because she said it got on her nerves. Do you know, sometimes on still, quiet evenings like this, I almost get a creepy feeling that they will all walk in through that window——'

She broke off with a little shudder. It was a relief to Framton when the aunt bustled into the room with a whirl of apologies for being late in making her appearance.

'I hope Vera has been amusing you?' she said.

'She has been very interesting,' said Framton.

'I hope you don't mind the open window,' said Mrs. Sappleton briskly; ' My husband and brothers will be home directly from shooting, and they always come in this way. They've been out for snipe in the marshes today, so they'll make a fine mess over my poor carpets. So like you men-folk isn't it?'

She rattled on cheerfully about the shooting and the scarcity of birds, and the prospects for duck in the winter. To Framton it was all purely horrible. He made a desperate but only partially successful effort to turn the talk on to a less ghastly topic; he was conscious that his hostess was giving him only a fragment of her attention, and her eyes were constantly straying past him to the open window and the lawn beyond. It was certainly an unfortunate coincidence that he should have paid his visit on this tragic anniversary.

'The doctors agree in ordering me complete rest, an absence of mental excitement, and avoidance of anything in the nature of violent physical exercise,' announced Framton, who laboured under the tolerably widespread delusion that total strangers and chance acquaintances are hungry for the least detail of one's ailments and infirmities, their cause and cure. 'On the matter of diet they are not so much in agreement,' he continued.

'No?' said Mrs. Sappleton, in a voice which only replaced a yawn at the last moment. Then she suddenly brightened into alert attention—but not to what Framton was saying.

'Here they are at last!' she cried. 'Just in time for tea, and don't they look as if they were muddy up to the eyes!'

Framton shivered slightly and turned towards the niece with a look intended to convey sympathetic comprehension. The child was staring out through the open window with dazed horror in her eyes. In a chill shock of nameless fear, Framton swung round in his seat and looked in the same direction.

In the deepening twilight three figures were walking across the lawn towards the window; they all carried guns under their arms, and one of them was additionally burdened with a white coat hung over his shoulders. A tired brown spaniel kept close at their heels. Noiselessly they neared the house, and then a hoarse young voice chanted out of the dusk: 'I said, Bertie, why do you bound?'

Framton grabbed wildly at his stick and hat; the hall-door, the gravel-drive, and the front gate were dimly noted stages in his headlong retreat. A cyclist coming along the road had to run into the hedge to avoid imminent collision.

'Here we are, my dear,' said the bearer of the white mackintosh, coming in through the window; 'fairly muddy, but

most of it's dry. Who was that who bolted out as we came
up?'

' A most extraordinary man, a Mr. Nuttel,' said Mrs.
Sappleton; 'could only talk about his illnesses, and dashed off
without a word of good-bye or apology when you arrived.
One would think he had seen a ghost.'

'I expect it was the spaniel,' said the niece calmly, 'he told
me he had a horror of dogs. He was once hunted into a
cemetery somewhere on the banks of the Ganges by a pack of
pariah dogs, and had to spend the night in a newly dug grave
with the creatures snarling and grinning and foaming just
above him. Enough to make anyone lose their nerve.'

Romance at short notice was her speciality.

Liam O'Flaherty

LIAM O'FLAHERTY was born in the Aran Islands of County Galway. He served in the First World War and with the Republican Army in the Irish Civil War.

He has travelled widely in most parts of the world, often working his passage. Among other things he has been a porter, a clerk, a lumberjack, a copper miner, and a dock labourer.

At one time he tried politics, but was soon disillusioned. Now he spends his time, so he says, 'writing, rearing Kerry goats, playing the melodeon and shaming the devil'.

His stories are filled with imagination and sympathy, and have a delicate, almost lyric quality.

THE REAPERS

AT DAWN the reapers were already in the rye field. It was the big rectangular field owned by James McDara, the retired engineer. The field started on the slope of the hill and ran down gently to the sea-road that was covered with sand. It was bound by a low stone fence, and the yellow heads of the rye-stalks leaned out over the fence, all round in a thick mass, jostling and crushing one another as the morning breeze swept over them with a swishing sound.

McDara himself, a white-haired old man in grey tweeds, was standing outside the fence on the sea-road, waving his stick and talking to a few people who had gathered even at that early hour. His brick-red face was all excitement, and he waved his blackthorn stick as he talked in a loud voice to the men about him.

'I measured it out yesterday,' he was saying, 'as even as it could be done. Upon my honour there isn't an inch in the difference between one strip and another of the three strips. D'ye see? I have laid lines along the length of the field so they can't go wrong. Come here and I'll show ye.'

He led the men along from end to end of the field and showed how he had measured it off into three even parts and marked the strips with lines laid along the ground.

'Now, it couldn't be fairer,' cried the old man as excited as a schoolboy. 'When I fire my revolver they'll all start together and the first couple to finish their strip gets a five-pound note.'

The peasants nodded their heads and looked at old McDara seriously, although each one of them thought he was crazy to spend five pounds on the cutting of a field that could be cut for two pounds. They were, however, almost as excited as McDara himself, for the three best reapers in the whole island of Inverara had entered for the competition. They were now at the top of the field on the slope of the hill ready to commence. Each had his wife with him to tie the sheaves as they were cut and bring food and drink.

They had cast lots for the strips by drawing three pieces of seaweed from McDara's hat. Now they had taken up position on their strips awaiting the signal. Although the sun had not yet warmed the earth and the sea breeze was cold, each man had stripped to his shirt. The shirts were open at the chest and the sleeves were rolled above the elbow. They wore grey woollen shirts. Around his waist each had a multi-coloured 'crios', a long knitted belt made of pure wool. Below that they wore white frieze drawers with the ends tucked into woollen stockings that were embroidered at the tops. Their feet were protected by raw-hide shoes. None of them wore a cap. The women all wore red petticoats, with a little shawl tied around their heads.

On the left were Michael Gill and his wife, Susan. Michael

was a long wiry man, with fair hair that came down over his forehead and was cropped to the bone all round the skull. He had a hook nose, and his lean jaws were continually moving backwards and forwards. His little blue eyes were fixed on the ground, and his long white lashes almost touched his cheekbones, as if he slept. He stood motionless, with his reaping hook in his right hand and his left hand in his belt. Now and again he lifted his eyelashes, listening for the signal to commence. His wife was almost as tall as himself, but she was plump and rosy-cheeked. A silent woman, she stood there thinking of her eight-months-old son whom she had left at home in charge of her mother.

In the middle Johnny Bodkin stood with his arms folded and his legs spread wide apart, talking to his wife in a low serious voice. He was a huge man, with fleshy limbs and neck, and black hair that had gone bald over his forehead. His forehead was very white and his cheeks were very red. He always frowned, twitching his black eyebrows. His wife, Mary, was short, thin, sallow-faced, and her upper teeth protruded slightly over her lower lip.

On the right was Pat Considine and his wife, Kate. Kate was very big and brawny, with a freckled face and a very marked moustache on her upper lip. She had a great mop of sandy-coloured curly hair that kept coming undone. She talked to her husband in a loud, gruff, masculine voice, full of good humour. Her husband, on the other hand, was a small man, small and slim, and beginning to get wrinkles in his face, although he was not yet forty. His face had once been a brick-red colour, but now it was becoming sallow. He had lost most of his front teeth. He stood loosely, grinning towards McDara, his little loose, slim body hiding its strength.

Then McDara waved his stick. He lifted his arm. A shot rang out. The reaping race began. In one movement the three men sank to their right knees like soldiers on parade at musketry practice. Their left hands closed in the same movement about a bunch of rye-stalks. The curved reaping hooks whirled in the air, and then there was a crunching sound, the sound that hungry cows make eating long fresh grass in spring. Then three little slender bunches of rye-stalks lay flat on the dewy grass beneath the fence, one bunch behind each reaper's bent left leg. The three women waited in nervous silence for the first sheaf. It would be an omen of victory or defeat. One, two, three, four bunches . . . Johnny Bodkin, snorting like a furious horse, was dropping his bunches almost without stopping. With a loud cheer he raised his reaping hook in the air and spat on it, crying, 'First sheaf!' His wife dived at it with both hands. Separating a little bunch of stalks, she encircled the head of the sheaf and then bound it with amazing rapidity, her long thin fingers moving like knitting needles. The other reapers and their wives had not paused to look. All three reapers had cut their first sheaves and their wives were on their knees tying.

Working in the same furious manner in which he had begun, Bodkin was soon far ahead of his competitors. He was cutting his sheaves in an untidy manner, and he was leaving hummocks behind him on the ground owing to the irregularities of his strokes, but his speed and strength were amazing. His great hand whirled the hook and closed on the stalks in a ponderous manner, and his body hurtled along like the carcass of an elephant trotting through a forest, but there was rhythm in the never-ending movement of his limbs that was not without beauty. And behind came his wife, tying, tying speedily, with her hard face gathered together in a serious frown like a person meditating on a grave decision.

Considine and his wife were second. Considine, now that he was in action, showed surprising strength and an agility that was goat-like. When his lean, long, bony arms moved to slash

the rye, muscles sprang up all over his bent back like an intricate
series of springs being pressed. Every time he hopped on his
right knee to move along his line of reaping he emitted a sound
like a groan cut short. His wife, already perspiring heavily,
worked almost on his heels, continually urging him on, laughing and joking in her habitual loud hearty voice.

Michael Gill and his wife came last. Gill had begun to reap
with the slow methodic movements of a machine driven at low
pressure. He continued at exactly the same pace, never changing, never looking up to see where his opponents were. His
long lean hands moved noiselessly, and only the sharp crunching rush of the teeth of his reaping hook through the yellow
stalks of the rye could be heard. His long drooping eyelids were
always directed towards the point where his hook was cutting.
He never looked behind to see if he had enough for a sheaf
before beginning another. All his movements were calculated
beforehand, calm, monotonous, deadly accurate. Even his
breathing was like, and came through his nose like one who
sleeps healthily. His wife moved behind him in the same
manner, tying each sheaf daintily, without exertion.

As the day advanced people gathered from all quarters watching the reapers. The sun rose into the heavens. There was a
fierce heat. Not a breath of wind. The rye-stalks no longer
moved. They stood in perfect silence, their heads a whitish
colour, their stalks golden. Already there was a large irregular
gash in the rye, ever increasing. The bare patch, green with little
clover plants that had been sown with the rye, was dotted with
sheaves, already whitening in the hot sun. Through the hum of
conversation the regular crunching of the reaping hooks could
be heard.

A little before noon Bodkin had cut half his strip. A stone
had been placed on the marking line at half way, and when
Bodkin reached the stone he stood up with the stone in his

hand and yelled: 'This is a proof,' he cried, 'that there was never a man born in the island of Inverara as good as Johnny Bodkin.' There was an answering cheer from the crowd on the fence, but big Kate Considine humorously waved a sheaf above her head and yelled in her rough man's voice: 'The day is young yet, Bodkin of the soft flesh!' The crowd roared with laughter, and Bodkin fumed, but he did not reply. His wits were not very sharp. Gill and his wife took no notice. They did not raise their eyes from the reaping.

Bodkin's wife was the first to go for the midday meal. She brought a can full of cold tea and a whole oven cake of white flour, cut in large pieces, each piece coated heavily with butter. She had four eggs, too, boiled hard. The Bodkin couple had no children, and on that account they could afford to live well, at least far better than the other peasants. Bodkin just dropped his reaping hook and ravenously devoured three of the eggs, while his wife, no less hungrily, ate the fourth. Then Bodkin began to eat the bread and butter and drink the cold tea with as much speed as he had reaped the rye. It took him and his wife exactly two minutes and three-quarters to finish that great quantity of food and drink. Out of curiosity, Gallagher, the doctor, counted the time down on the shore-road. As soon as they had finished eating they set to work again as fiercely as ever.

Considine had come level with Bodkin, just as Bodkin resumed work, and instead of taking a rest for their meal, Considine and his wife ate in the ancient fashion current among Inverara peasants during contests of the kind. Kate fed her husband as he worked with buttered oaten cake. Now and then she handed him the tea-can and he paused to take a drink. In that way he was still almost level with Bodkin when he had· finished eating. The spectators were greatly excited at this eagerness on the part of Considine, and some began to say that he would win the race.

Nobody took any notice of Gill and his wife, but they had never stopped to eat, and they had drawn steadily nearer to their opponents. They were still some distance in the rear, but they seemed quite fresh, whereas Bodkin appeared to be handicapped by his heavy meal, and Considine was obviously using up the reserves of his strength. Then, when they reached the stone at half way, Gill quietly laid down his hook and told his wife to bring the meal. She brought it from the fence, buttered oaten bread and a bottle of new milk, with oatmeal in the bottom of the bottle. They ate slowly, and then rested for a while. People began to jeer at them when they saw them resting, but they took no notice. After about twenty minutes they got up to go to work again. A derisive cheer arose, and an old man cried out: 'Yer a disgrace to me name, Michael.'

'Never mind, father,' called Michael, 'the race isn't finished yet.' Then he spat on his hands and seized his hook once more.

Then, indeed, excitement rose to a high pitch, because the Gill couple resumed work at a great speed. Their movements were as mechanical and regular as before, but they worked at almost twice the speed. People began to shout at them. Then betting began among the gentry. Until now the excitement had not been intense because it seemed a foregone conclusion that Bodkin would win since he was so far ahead. Now, however, Bodkin's supremacy was challenged. He still was a long way ahead of Gill, but he was visibly tired, and his hook made mistakes now and again, gripping the earth with its point. Bodkin was lathered with sweat. He now began to look behind him at Gill, irritated by the shouts of the people.

Just before four o'clock Considine suddenly collapsed, utterly exhausted. He had to be carried over to the fence. A crowd gathered around, and the rector, Mr. Robertson, gave him a swig from his brandy flask and revived him. He made an effort to go back to work, but he was unable to rise. 'Stay there,' said his wife angrily, 'you're finished. I'll carry on myself.' Rolling up her sleeves further on her fat arms, she went back to the reaping hook, and with a loud yell began to reap furiously. 'Bravo,' cried McDara, 'I'll give the woman a special prize. Gallagher,' he cried, hitting the doctor on the shoulder, 'after all . . . the Irish race . . . ye know what I mean . . . man, alive.'

But all centred their attention on the struggle between Bodkin and Gill. Spurred by rage, Bodkin had made a supreme effort, and he began to gain ground once more. His immense body, moving from left to right and back again across his line of reaping, seemed to swallow the long yellow rye-stalks, so quickly did they fall before it. And as the sheaf was complete his lean wife grabbed it up and tied it. But still, when Bodkin paused at five o'clock to cast a look behind him, there was Gill coming with terrible regularity. Bodkin suddenly felt all the weariness of the day overcome him.

It struck him first in the shape of an intense thirst. He sent his wife up to the fence for their extra can of tea. When she came back with it he began to drink. But the more he drank the thirstier he became. His friends in the crowd of spectators shouted at him in warning, but his thirst maddened him. He kept drinking. The shore-wall and victory were very near now. He kept looking towards it in a dazed way as he whirled his hook. And he kept drinking. Then his senses began to dull. He became sleepy. His movements became almost unconscious. He only saw the wall and he fought on. He began to talk to himself. He reached the wall at one end of his strip. He had only to cut down to the other end and finish. Three sheaves more, and then. . . . Best man in Inverara. . . . Five-pound note. . . .

But just then a ringing cheer came to his ears, and the cry rose in the air: 'Gill has won.' Bodkin collapsed with a groan.

William Sansom

Not until he was over thirty years old did William Sansom decide to make writing his full-time career. Before that he tried banking advertising, and filming. On the continent he worked as a director of radio programmes.

Handsome and bearded, he is now married to an actress, Ruth Grundy, and lives in London.

He is recognized as one of our leading short-story writers and his work has been published throughout the world in many languages.

THE VERTICAL LADDER

AS HE felt the first watery eggs of sweat moistening the palms of his hands, as with every rung higher his body seemed to weigh more heavily, this young man Flegg regretted in sudden desperation, but still in vain, the irresponsible events that had thrust him up into his present precarious climb. Here he was, isolated on a vertical iron ladder flat to the side of a gasometer and bound to climb higher and higher until he could reach the vertiginous skyward summit.

How could he ever have wished this on himself? How easy it had been to laugh away his cautionary fears on the ground ... now he would give the very hands that clung to the ladder for a safe conduct to solid earth.

It had been a strong spring day, abruptly as warm as midsummer. The sun flooded the parks and streets with sudden heat—Flegg and his friends had felt stifled in their thick winter clothes. The green glare of the new leaves everywhere struck the eye too fiercely, the air seemed almost sticky from the exhalations of buds and swelling resins. Cold winter senses

were overcome—the girls had complained of headaches—and
their thoughts had grown confused and uncomfortable as the
wool underneath against their skins. They had wandered out
from the park by a back gate, into an area of back streets.

The houses there were small and old, some of them already
falling into disrepair, short streets, cobbles, narrow pavements,
and the only shops a tobacconist or a desolate corner oil-shop
to colour the grey—it was the outcrop of some industrial
undertaking beyond. At first these quiet, almost deserted streets
had seemed more restful than the park; but soon a dusty air of
peeling plaster and powdering brick, the dark windows and the
dry stone steps, the very dryness altogether had proved more
wearying than before, so that when suddenly the houses ended
and the ground opened to reveal the yards of a disused gasworks, Flegg and his friends had welcomed the green of nettles
and milkwort that grew among the scrap-iron and broken
brick.

They walked out into the wasteland, the two girls and Flegg
and the other two boys, and stood presently before the old
gasometer itself. Among the ruined sheds this was the only
erection still whole, it still predominated over the yards, tower-
ing high above other buildings for hundreds of feet around.
So they threw bricks against its rusted sides.

The rust flew off in flakes and the iron rang dully. Flegg,
who wished to excel in the eyes of the dark-haired girl, began
throwing his bricks higher than the others, at the same time
lobbing them, to suggest that he knew something of grenade-
throwing, claiming for himself vicariously the glamour of a
uniform. He felt the girl's eyes follow his shoulders, his
shoulders broadened. She had black eyes, unshadowed beneath
short wide-awake lids, as bright as a boy's eyes; her lips pouted
with difficulty over a scramble of irregular teeth, so that it
often looked as if she were laughing; she always frowned—and

Flegg liked her earnest, purposeful expression. Altogether she seemed a wide-awake girl who would be the first to appreciate an active sort of man. Now she frowned and shouted: 'Bet you can't climb as high as you can throw!'

Then there began one of those uneasy jokes, innocent at first, that taken seriously can accumulate an hysterical accumulation of spite. Everyone recognizes this underlying unpleasantness, it is plainly felt; but just because of this the joke must at all costs be pressed forward, one becomes frightened, one laughs all the louder, pressing to drown the embarrassments of danger and guilt. The third boy had instantly shouted: 'Course he can't, he can't climb no higher than himself.'

Flegg turned round scoffing, so that the girl had quickly shouted again, laughing shrilly and pointing upwards. Already all five of them felt uneasy. Then in quick succession, all in a few seconds, the third boy had repeated: 'Course he b—— can't.' Flegg had said: 'Climb to the top of anything.' The other boy had said: 'Climb to the top of my aunt Fanny.' The girl had said: 'Climb to the top of the gasworks then.'

Flegg had said: 'That's nothing.' And the girl, pressing on then as she had to, suddenly introduced the inevitable detail that made these suppositions into fact: 'Go on then, climb it. Here—tie my hanky on the top. Tie my flag to the top.'

Even then Flegg had a second's chance. It occurred to him instantly that he could laugh it off; but an hysterical emphasis now possessed the girl's face—she was dancing up and down and clapping her hands insistently—and this confused Flegg. He began stuttering after the right words. But the words refused to come. At all costs he had to cover his stuttering. So: 'Off we go then!' he had said. And he had turned to the gasometer.

It was not, after all, so very high. It was hardly a full-size gasometer, its trellised iron top-rail would have stood level with the roof-coping of a five- or six-storey tenement. Until then Flegg had only seen the gasometer as a rough mass of iron, but now every detail sprang into abrupt definition. He studied it intently, alertly considering its size and every feature of stability, the brown rusted iron sheeting smeared here and there with red lead, a curious buckling that sometimes deflated its curved bulk as though a vacuum were collapsing it from within, and the ladders scaling the sides flush with the sheeting. The grid of girders, the complexity of struts, the bolting.

There were two ladders, one Jacob's ladder clamped fast to the side, another that was more of a staircase, zigzagging up the belly of the gasometer in easy gradients and provided with a safety rail. This must have been erected later as a substitute for the Jacob's ladder, which demanded an unnecessarily stringent climb and was now in fact in disuse, for some twenty feet of its lower rungs had been torn away; however, there was some painting in progress, for a painter's wooden ladder had been propped beneath with its head reaching to the undamaged bottom of the vertical ladder—the ascent was thus serviceable again. Flegg looked quickly at the foot of the wooden ladder—was it well grounded?—and then at the head farther up—was this secure?—and then up to the top, screwing his eyes to note any fault in the iron rungs reaching innumerably and indistinctly, like the dizzying strata of a zip, to the summit platform.

Flegg, rapidly assessing these structures, never stopped sauntering forward. He was committed, and so while deliberately sauntering to appear thus the more at ease, he knew that he must never hesitate. The two boys and his own girl kept up a chorus of encouraging abuse. 'How I climbed Mount Everest,' they shouted. 'He'll come down quicker'n he went up.' ' Mind you don't bang your head on a harp, Sir Galahad.' But the second girl had remained quiet throughout, she was already frightened, sensing instantly that the guilt for some tragedy was hers alone—although she had never in fact opened her mouth. Now she chewed passionately on gum that kept her jaws firm and circling.

Suddenly the chorus rose shriller. Flegg had veered slightly towards the safer staircase. His eyes had naturally questioned this along with the rest of the gasometer, and almost unconsciously his footsteps had veered in the direction of his eye; then his instinct had emerged into full consciousness—perhaps he could use the staircase, no one had actually instanced the Jacob's ladder, there might yet be a chance? But the quick eyes behind had seen him, and immediately the chorus rose: 'No you don't!' 'Not up those cissy stairs!' Flegg switched his course by only the fraction that turned him again to the perpendicular ladder. 'Who's talking about stairs?' he shouted back.

Behind him they still kept up a din, still kept him to pitch, worrying at him viciously. 'Look at him, he doesn't know which way to go—he's like a ruddy duck's uncle without an aunt.'

So that Flegg realized that there was no alternative. He had to climb the gasometer by the vertical ladder. And as soon as this was finally settled, the doubt cleared from his mind. He braced his shoulders and suddenly found himself making really light of the job. After all, he thought, it isn't so high. Why should I worry? Hundreds of men climb such ladders each day, no one falls, the ladders are clamped as safe as houses! He began to smile within himself at his earlier perturbations. Added to this, the girl now ran up to him and handed him her handkerchief. As her black eyes frowned a smile at him, he saw that her expression no longer held its vicious laughing scorn, but now instead had grown softer, with a look of real encouragement and even admiration. 'Here's your flag,' she said. And then she even added: 'Tell you what—you don't really have to go! I'll believe you!' But this came too late. Flegg had accepted the climb, it was fact, and already he felt something of an exhilarating glow of glory. He took the handkerchief, blew the girl a dramatic kiss, and started up the lowest rungs of the ladder at a run.

This painter's ladder was placed at a comfortable slant. But nevertheless Flegg had only climbed some ten feet—what might have corresponded to the top of a first-floor window— when he began to slow up; he stopped running and gripped harder at the rungs above and placed his feet more firmly on the unseen bars below. Although he had not yet measured his distance from the ground, somehow he sensed distinctly that he was already unnaturally high, with nothing but air and a precarious skeleton of wooden bars between him and the receding ground. He felt independent of solid support: yet, according to his eyes, which stared straight forward at the iron sheeting beyond, he might have been still standing on the lowest rungs by the ground. The sensation of height infected him strongly, it had become an urgent necessity to maintain a balance, each muscle of his body became unnaturally alert. This was not an unpleasant feeling, he almost enjoyed a new athletic command of every precarious movement. He climbed them methodically until he reached the ladderhead and the first of the perpendicular iron rungs.

Here for a moment Flegg had paused. He had rested his knees up against the last three steps of the safety-slanting wooden ladder, he had grasped the two side supports of the rusted iron that led so straightly upwards. His knees then clung to the motherly wood, his hands felt the iron cold and gritty. The rust powdered off and smeared him with its red dust; one large scrap flaked off and fell on his face as he looked upwards.

He wanted to brush this away from his eye, but the impulse was, to his surprise, much less powerful than the vice-like will that clutched his hands to the iron support. His hand remained firmly gripping the iron, he had to shake off the rust-flake with a jerk of his head. Even then this sharp movement nearly unbalanced him, and his stomach gulped coldly with the sudden shock. He settled his knees more firmly against the wood, and though he forced himself to laugh at this sudden fear, so that in some measure his poise did really return, nevertheless he did not alter the awkward knock-kneed position of his legs patently clinging for safety. With all this he had scarcely paused. Now he pulled at the stanchions of the iron ladder, they were as firm as if they had been driven into rock.

He looked up, following the dizzying rise of the rungs to the skyline. From this angle flat against the iron sheeting, the gasometer appeared higher than before. The blue sky seemed to descend and almost touch it. The redness of the rust dissolved into a deepening grey shadow, the distant curved summit loomed over black and high. Although it was immensely stable, as seen in rounded perspective from a few yards away, there against the side it appeared top heavy, so that this huge segment of sheet iron seemed to have lost the support of its invisible complement behind, the support that was now unseen and therefore unfelt, and Flegg imagined despite himself that the entire erection had become unsteady, that quite possibly the gasometer might suddenly blow over like a gigantic top-heavy sail. He lowered his eyes quickly and concentrated on the hands before him. He began to climb.

From beneath him there still rose a few cries from the boys. But the girl had stopped shouting—probably she was following Flegg's every step with admiring eyes. He imagined again her frown and her peculiarly pouting mouth, and from this image drew new strength with which he clutched the rungs more

eagerly. But now he noticed that the cries had begun to ring
with an unpleasant echo, as though they were already far off.
And Flegg could not so easily distinguish their words. Even
at this height he seemed to have penetrated into a distinct
strata of separate air, for it was certainly cooler, and for the
first time that day he felt the light fanning of a wind. He
looked down. His friends appeared shockingly small. Their
bodies had disappeared and he saw only their upturned faces.
He wanted to wave, to demonstrate in some way a carefree
attitude; but then instantly he felt frustrated as his hands refused
to unlock their grip. He turned to the rungs again with the
smile dying on his lips. He swallowed uneasily and continued
to tread slowly upwards, hand after hand, foot after foot. He
had climbed ten rungs of the iron ladder when his hands first
began to feel moist, when suddenly, as though a catastrophe
had overtaken him not gradually but in one overpowering
second, he realized that he was afraid; incontrovertibly. He
could cover it no longer, he admitted it all over his body. His
hands gripped with pitiable eagerness, they were now alert to a
point of shivering, as though the nerves inside them had been
forced taut for so long that now they had burst beyond their
strained tegument; his feet no longer trod firmly on the rungs
beneath, but first stepped for their place timorously, then
glued themselves to the iron. In this way his body lost much
of its poise; these nerves and muscles in his two legs and two
arms seemed to work independently, no longer integrated with
the rhythm of his body, but moving with the dangerous
unwilling jerk of crippled limbs.

His body hung slack away from the ladder, with nothing
beneath it but a thirty foot drop to the ground; only his hands
and feet were fed with the security of an attachment, most of
him lay off the ladder, hanging in space; his arms revolted at
the strain of their unfamiliar angle, as though they were flies'

feet denying all natural laws. For the first time, as the fear took hold of him, he felt that what he had attempted was impossible. He could never achieve the top. If at this height of only thirty feet, as it were three storeys of a building, he felt afraid— what would he feel at sixty feet? Yet . . . he trod heavily up. He was afraid, but not desperate. He dreaded each step, yet forced himself to believe that at some time it would be over, it could not take long.

But ten rungs further up he began to sweat more violently than ever. His hands streamed with wet rust, the flesh inside his thighs blenched. Another flake of rust fell on his forehead; this time it stuck in the wetness. He felt physically exhausted. Fear was draining his strength and the precarious position of his body demanded an awkward physical effort. From his outstretched arms suspended most of the weight of his body. Each stressed muscle ached. His body weighed more heavily at each step upwards, it sagged beneath his arms like a leaden sack. His legs no longer provided their adequate support; it seemed as though they needed every pull of their muscle to force themselves, as independent limbs, close to the ladder. The wind blew faster. It dragged now at his coat, it blew its space about him, it echoed silently a lonely spaciousness. 'Don't look down,' the blood whispered in his temples, 'Don't look down, for God's sake, DON'T LOOK DOWN.'

Three-quarters up the gasometer, and fifty feet from the ground, Flegg grew desperate. Every other consideration suddenly left him. He wanted only to reach the ground as quickly as possible, only that. Nothing else mattered. He stopped climbing and clung to the ladder panting. Very slowly, lowering his eyes carefully so that he could raise them instantly if he saw too much, he looked down a rung, and another, past his armpit, past his waist—and focused them on the ground beneath. He looked quickly up again.

He pressed himself to the ladder. Tears started in his eyes. For a moment they reeled red with giddiness. He closed them, shutting out everything. Then instantly opened them, afraid that something might happen. He must watch his hands, watch the bars, watch the rusted iron sheeting itself; no movement should escape him; the struts might come creaking loose, the whole edifice might sway over; although a fading reason told him that the gasometer had remained firm for years and was still as steady as a cliff, his horrified senses suspected that this was the one moment in the building's life when a wind would blow that was too strong for it, some defective strut would snap, the whole edifice would heel over and go crashing to the ground. This image became so clear that he could see the sheets of iron buckling and folding like cloth as the huge weight sank to the earth.

The ground had receded horribly, the drop now appeared terrifying, out of all proportion to the height he had reached. From the ground such a height would have appeared unnoteworthy. But now looking down the distance seemed to have doubled. Each object familiar to his everyday eyes—his friends, the lamp-posts, a brick wall, the kerb, a drain—all these had grown infinitely small. His senses demanded that these objects should be of a certain accustomed size. Alternatively the world of chimneys and attic windows and roof copings would grow unpleasantly giant as his pavement-bred eyes approached. Even now the iron sheeting that stretched to either side and above and below seemed to have grown, he was lost among such huge smooth dimensions, grown smaller himself and clinging now like a child lost on some monstrous desert of red dust.

These unfamiliarities shocked his nerves more than the danger of falling. The sense of isolation was overpowering. All things were suddenly alien. Yet exposed on the iron spaces with the unending winds blowing aerially round him, among such free things—he felt shut in! Trembling and panting so that he stifled himself with the shortness of his own breath, he took the first step downwards. . . .

A commotion began below. A confusion of cries came drifting up to him. Above all he could hear the single voice of the girl who had so far kept quiet. She was screaming high, a shrill scream that rose incisively like a gull's shriek. 'Put it back, put it back, put it back!' the scream seemed to say. So that Flegg, thinking that these cries were to warn him of some new danger apparent only from the ground—Flegg gripped himself to the ladder and looked down again. He glanced down only for a fractional second—but in that time saw enough. He saw the quiet girl was screaming and pointing to the base of the iron ladder. He saw the others crowding round her, gesticulating. He saw what she really had been crying, 'Put it back!' And he realized now what the words meant—someone had removed the painter's ladder.

It lay clearly on the ground, outlined white like a child's drawing of a ladder. The boys must have seen his first step downwards, and then, from fun or from spite they had removed his only means of retreat. He remembered that from the base of the iron ladder to the ground the drop fell twenty feet. He considered quickly descending and appealing from the bottom of the ladder; but foresaw that for precious minutes they would bicker and argue, refusing to replace the ladder, and he felt then that he could never risk these minutes, unnerved, with his strength failing. Besides, he had already noticed that the whole group of them were wandering off. The boys were driving the quiet girl away, now more concerned with her than with Flegg. The quiet girl's sense of guilt had been brought to a head by the removal of the ladder. Now she was hysterically terrified. She was yelling to them to put the ladder back. She—only she, the passive one—sensed the terror that awaited them all. But her screams defeated their own purpose. They had altogether distracted the attention of the others; now it was fun to provoke more screams, to encourage this new distraction—and they forgot about Flegg far up and beyond them. They were wandering away. They were abandoning him, casually unconcerned that he was alone and helpless up in his wide prison of rust. His heart cried out for them to stay. He forgot their scorn in new and terrible torments of self-pity. An uneasy feeling lumped his throat, his eyes smarted with dry tears.

But they were wandering away. There was no retreat. They did not even know he was in difficulties. So Flegg had no option but to climb higher. Desperately he tried to shake off his fear, he actually shook his head. Then he stared hard at the rungs immediately facing his eyes, and tried to imagine that he was not high at all. He lifted himself tentatively by one rung, then by another, and in this way dragged himself higher and higher . . . until he must have been some ten rungs from the top, over the fifth storey of a house, with now perhaps only one more storey to climb. He imagined that he might then be approaching the summit platform, and to measure this last distance he looked up.

He looked up and heaved. He felt for the first time panicked beyond desperation, wildly, violently loose. He almost let go, yet his hands refused to open. He was stretched on a rack made by these hands that would not unlock their grip and by the panic desire to drop. The nerves left his hands, so that they might have been dried bones of fingers gripped round the rungs, hooks of bone fixed perhaps strongly enough to cling on, or perhaps ready at some moment of pressure to uncurl their vertebrae and straighten to a drop. His insteps pricked with cold cramp. The sweat sickened him. His loins seemed to empty themselves. His trousers ran wet. He shivered, grew giddy, and flung himself froglike on to the ladder.

The sight of the top of the gasometer had proved endemically more frightful that the appearance of the drop beneath. There lay about it a sense not of material danger, not of the risk of falling, but of something removed and unhuman—a sense of appalling isolation. It echoed its elemental iron aloofness, a wind blew round it that had never known the warmth of flesh nor the softness of green fibres. Its blind eyes were raised above the world. It might have been the eyeless iron visor of an ancient God. It touched against the sky, having risen in awful perpendicular to this isolation, solitary as the grey gannet cliffs that mark the end of the northern world. It was immeasurably old, outside the connotation of time; it was nothing human, only washed by the high weather, echoing with wind, visited never and silently alone.

And in this summit Flegg measured clearly the full distance of his climb. This close skyline emphasised the whirling space beneath him. He clearly saw a man fall through this space, spread-eagling to smash with the sickening force of a locomotive on the stone beneath. The man turned slowly in the air, yet his thoughts raced faster than he fell.

Flegg, clutching his body close to the rust, made small weeping sounds through his mouth. Shivering, shuddering, he began to tread up again, working his knees and elbows outwards like a frog, so that his stomach could feel the firm rungs. Were they firm? His ears filled with a hot roaring, he hurried himself, he began to scramble up, wrenching at his last strength, whispering urgent meaningless words to himself like the swift whispers that close in on a nightmare. A huge weight pulled at him, dragging him to the top. He climbed higher. He reached the top rung—and found his face staring still at a wall of rust. He looked, wild with terror. It was the top rung! The ladder

had ended! Yet—no platform . . . the real top rungs were
missing . . . the platform jutted five impassable feet above. . . .
Flegg stared dumbly, circling his head like a lost animal . . .
then he jammed his legs in the lower rungs and his arms past
the elbows to the armpits in through the top rungs and there
he hung shivering and past knowing what more he could
ever do. . . .

Giovanni Guareschi

GIOVANNI GUARESCHI lives in the town of Parma near the River Po in Italy. Five feet ten inches tall, he has thick shining hair, and a heavy black moustache of which he is inordinately proud.

He left school to study law, and then took a succession of jobs as a doorman in a sugar refinery, a superintendent in a bicycle parking lot, a census taker and a teacher in a boarding school. He also became famous as a signboard writer. 'And,' he adds, 'since I knew nothing at all about music, I began to give mandoline lessons.'

Guareschi's mother taught in the local elementary school for nearly fifty years. His father, in his grander days, would travel around in an automobile, followed by cheering villagers excited at the wonder of the horseless carriage. When that period of grandeur passed, says Guareschi, his father attached the horn of the automobile (the kind you squeeze), to the head of the bed, and there he would lie honking, especially in the summer.

'I also have a brother,' Guareschi says, 'but I had an argument with him two weeks ago and prefer not to discuss him. I also have a motorcycle with four cylinders, an automobile with six cylinders, and a wife and two children.'

During the war he was taken prisoner by the Germans and sent to a concentration camp. There he adopted the slogan: 'I will not die, even if they kill me.'

The war over he returned to Italy where he worked for the magazine *Candido* which, he says, 'valued my contributions very highly—perhaps because I was editor-in-chief.'

It was in *Candido* that Guareschi introduced the lovable and muscular priest together with his great friend and adversary the Communist mayor.

A CONFESSION

DON CAMILLO had been born with a constitutional preference for calling a spade a spade. Upon a certain occasion when there had been a local scandal involving landowners of ripe age and young girls of his parish, he had, in the course of his mass, embarked on a seemly and suitably generalised address, when he had suddenly become aware of the fact that one of the chief offenders was present among the foremost ranks of his congregation. Flinging all restraint to the four winds and also flinging a hastily snatched cloth over the head of the Crucified Lord above the high altar in order that the divine ears might not be offended, he had set his arms firmly akimbo and had resumed his sermon. And so stentorian had been the voice that issued from the lips of the big man and so uncomprising had been his language that the very roof of the little church had seemed to tremble.

When the time of the elections drew near, Don Camillo had naturally been explicit in his allusions to the local leftists. Thus there came a fine evening when, as he was going home at dusk, an individual muffled in a cloak sprang out of a hedge as he passed by and, taking advantage of the fact that Don Camillo was handicapped by his bicycle and by a large parcel containing seventy eggs attached to its handlebars, belaboured him with a heavy stick and promptly vanished as though the earth had swallowed him.

Don Camillo had kept his own counsel. Having arrived at the presbytery and deposited the eggs in safety, he had gone into the church to discuss the matter with the Lord, as was his invariable habit in moments of perplexity.

'What should I do?' Don Camillo had inquired.

'Annoint your back with a little oil beaten up in water and

hold your tongue,' the Lord had replied from above the altar. 'We must forgive those who offend us. That is the rule.'

'Very true, Lord,' agreed Don Camillo, 'but on this occasion we are discussing blows, not offences.'

'And what do you mean by that? Surely you are not trying to tell me that injuries done to the body are more painful than those aimed at the spirit?'

'I see your point, Lord. But You should also bear in mind that in the beating of me, who am Your minister, an injury has been done to Yourself also. I am really more concerned on Your behalf than on my own.'

'And was I not a greater minister of God than you are? And did I not forgive those who nailed me to the Cross?'

'There is never any use in arguing with You!' Don Camillo had exxlaimed. 'You are always in the right. Your will be done. We must forgive. All the same, don't forget that if these ruffians, encouraged by my silence, should crack my skull, the responsibility will lie with You. I could cite several passages from the old Testament. . . .'

'Don Camillo, are you proposing to instruct me in the Old Testament? As for this business, I assume full responsibility. Moreover, strictly between Ourselves, the beating has done you no harm. It may teach you to let politics alone in my house.'

Don Camillo had duly forgiven. But nevertheless one thing stuck in his gullet like a fish bone: curiosity as to the identity of his assailant.

Time passed. Late one evening, while he sat in the confessional, Don Camillo discerned through the grille the countenance of the local leader of the extreme leftists, Peppone.

That Peppone should come to confession at all was a sensational event, and Don Camillo was proportionately gratified.

'God be with you, brother; with you, who, more than any

other man, have need of His holy blessing. It is a long time since you last went to confession?'

'Not since 1918,' replied Peppone.

'You must have committed a great number of sins in the course of those twenty-eight years, with your head so crammed with crazy notions. . . .'

'A good few, undoubtedly,' sighed Peppone.

'For example.'

'For example, two months ago I gave you a hiding.'

'That was serious indeed,' replied Don Camillo, 'since in assaulting a minister of God, you have attacked God Himself.'

'But I have repented,' exclaimed Peppone. 'And, moreover, it was not as God's minister that I beat you, but as my political adversary. In any case, I did it in a moment of weakness.'

'Apart from this and from your membership of your accursed Party, have you any other grave sins on your conscience?'

Peppone spilled all the beans.

Taken as a whole, his offences were not very serious, and Don Camillo let him off with a score of Paters and Aves. Then, while Peppone was kneeling at the altar rails performing his penance, Don Camillo went and knelt before the crucifix.

'Lord,' he said, 'You must forgive me, but I am going to beat him up for You.'

'You are going to do nothing of the kind,' replied the Lord. 'I have forgiven him and you must forgive him also. All things considered, he is not a bad soul.'

'Lord, you can never trust a Red! They live by lies. Only look at him; Barabbas incarnate!'

'It's as good a face as most, Don Camillo; it is your heart that is venomous!'

'Lord, if I have ever served You well, grant me just one small grace; let me at least break this candle on his shoulders. Dear Lord, what, after all, is a candle?'

'No,' replied the Lord. 'Your hands were made for blessing, not for striking.'

Don Camillo sighed heavily.

He genuflected and left the sanctuary. As he turned to make a final sign of the cross he found himself exactly behind Peppone, who, on his knees, was apparently absorbed in prayer.

'Lord,' groaned Don Camillo, clasping his hands and gazing at the crucifix, 'my hands were made for blessing, but not my feet!'

'There is something in that,' replied the Lord from above the altar, 'but all the same, Don Camillo, bear it in mind: only one!'

The kick landed like a thunderbolt and Peppone received it without so much as blinking an eye. Then he got to his feet and sighed with relief.

'I've been waiting for that for the last ten minutes,' he remarked. 'I feel better now.'

'So do I!' exclaimed Don Camillo, whose heart was as light and serene as a May morning.

The Lord said nothing at all, but it was easy enough to see that He too was pleased.

THE DEFEAT

THE WAR to the knife that had now been in process for nearly a year was won by Don Camillo, who managed to complete his recreation centre while Peppone's People's Palace still lacked all its locks.

The recreation centre proved to be a very up-to-date affair: a hall for social gatherings, dramatic performances, lectures and suchlike activities, a library with a reading and writing room and a covered area for physical training and winter games. There was in addition a magnificent fenced sports ground with a gymnasium, running-track, bathing-pool and a children's playground with giant-stride, swings, etcetera. Most of the paraphernalia was as yet in an embryonic stage, but the important thing was to have made a start.

For the inauguration ceremony Don Camillo had prepared a most lively programme: choral singing, athletic competitions, and a game of football. For the latter Don Camillo had succeeded in mustering a really formidable team, a task to which he had brought so impassioned an enthusiasm that in the course of the team's eight months of training the kicks administered by him alone to the eleven players were far more numerous than those that all those players put together had succeeded in giving to the ball.

Peppone knew all this and was deeply embittered. He could not endure the thought that the party that genuinely represented the people must play second fiddle in the celebration organized by Don Camillo on the people's behalf. And when Don Camillo sent to inform him that in order to demonstrate his 'sympathetic understanding of the more ignorant social strata of the village' he was willing to allow a match between their Dynamos football team and his own Galliards, Peppone turned pale, summoned the eleven lads of the local sports squadron and made them stand to attention against the wall while he made them the following address: 'You are to play against the priest's team. You have got to win or I shall smash in every one of your faces. The Party orders it for the honour of a downtrodden people!'

'We shall win!' replied the eleven, sweating with terror.

As soon as this scene was reported to him Don Camillo mustered the Galliards and addressed them as follows.

'We are not here among uncouth savages such as your

opponents,' he said, smiling pleasantly. 'We are capable of reasoning like sensible and educated gentlemen. With the help of God, we shall beat them six goals to none. I make no threats; I merely remind you that the honour of the parish is in your hands. Also in your feet.

'Therefore let each of you do his duty as a good citizen. Should there be some Barabbas among you who is not ready to give his all even to the last drop of his blood, I shall not indulge in Peppone's histrionics with regard to the smashing of faces. I shall merely kick his backside to a jelly!'

The entire countryside attended the inauguration, led by Peppone and his satellites with blazing red handkerchiefs around their necks. In his capacity as *mayor*, he expressed his satisfaction at the event, and as *personal representative of the people* he emphasized his confident belief that the occasion they were celebrating would not be made to serve 'unworthy ends of political propaganda such as were already being whispered of by ill-intentioned persons.'

During the performance of the choral singers, Peppone was able to point out to Brusco that, as a matter of fact, singing was also a sport, inasmuch as it developed the expansion of the lungs, and Brusco, with seeming amiability, replied that in his opinion the exercise would prove even more efficacious as a means of physical development for Catholic youth if they were taught to accompany it with gestures adapted to the improvement not only of their lung power, but also of the muscles of their arms.

During the game of basket-ball Peppone expressed a sincere conviction that the game of ping-pong also not only had an undeniable athletic value, but was so graceful that he was astonished not to find it included in the programme.

In view of the fact that these comments were made in voices that were easily audible half a mile away, the veins of Don

Camillo's neck were very soon swelled to the size of cables. He therefore waited with indescribable impatience the hour of the football match, which would be that of his reply.

At last it was time for the match. White jerseys with a large 'G' on the breast for the eleven Galliards. Red jerseys bearing the hammer, sickle, and star combined with an elegant 'D' adorned the eleven Dynamos.

The crowd cared less than nothing for symbols, anyway, and hailed the teams after their own fashion. 'Hurrah for Peppone!' or 'Hurrah for Don Camillo!' Peppone and Don Camillo looked at one another and exchanged slight and dignified bows.

The referee was a neutral: the clockmaker Binella, a man without political opinions. After ten minutes' play the sergeant of carabinieri, pale to the gills, approached Peppone, followed by his two equally pallid subordinates.

'Mr. Mayor,' he stammered, 'don't you think it would be wise for me to telephone to the town for reinforcements?'

'You can telephone for a division for all I care, but if those butchers don't let up, nobody will be able to avoid there being a heap of corpses as high as the first-floor windows! Not His Majesty the King himself could do a thing about it, do you understand?' howled Peppone, forgetting the very existence of the republic in his blind fury.

The sergeant turned to Don Camillo, who was standing a few feet away. 'Don't you think . . .?' he stuttered, but Don Camillo cut him short.

'I,' he shouted, 'simply think that nothing short of the personal intervention of the United States of America will prevent us all from swimming in blood if those accursed bolsheviks don't stop disabling my men by kicking them in the shins!'

'I see,' said the sergeant, and went off to barricade himself into his quarters, although perfectly aware that the common sequel of such behaviour is a general attempt to close the festivities by setting fire to the barracks of the carabinieri.

The first goal was scored by the Galliards and raised a howl that shook the church tower. Peppone, his face distorted with rage, turned on Don Camillo with clenched fists as though about to attack him. Don Camillo's fists were already in position. The two of them were within a hair's-breadth of conflict, but Don Camillo observed out of the tail of his eye that all other eyes present were fixed on them.

'If we begin fighting there'll be a free-for-all,' he muttered through clenched teeth to Peppone.

'All right, for the sake of the people.'

'For the sake of the faith,' said Don Camillo.

Nothing happened. Nevertheless, Peppone, when the first half ended a few moments later, mustered the Dynamos. 'Fascists!' he said to them in a voice thick with contempt. Then, seizing hold of Smilzo, the centre-forward: 'As for you, you dirty traitor, suppose you remember that when we were in the mountains I saved your worthless skin no less than three times. If in the next five minutes you haven't scored a goal, I'll attend to that same skin of yours.'

Smilzo, when play was resumed, got the ball and set to work. And work he did, with his head, with his legs, and with his knees. He even bit the ball, he spat his lungs out and split his spleen, but the fourth minute he sent the ball between the posts.

Then he flung himself on to the ground and lay motionless. Don Camillo moved over to the other side of the ground lest his self-control should fail him. The Galliards' goalkeeper was in a high fever from sheer funk.

The Dynamos closed up into a defensive phalanx that seemed impregnable. Thirty seconds before the next break the referee whistled and a penalty was given against the Galliards. The ball flew into the air. A child of six could not have muffed it at such an angle. Goal!

The match was now over. The only task remaining for Peppone's men was that of picking up their injured players and carrying them back to their pavilion. The referee had no political views and left them to it.

Don Camillo was bewildered. He ran off to the church and knelt in front of the altar. 'Lord,' he said, 'why did You fail to help me? I have lost the match.'

'And why should I have helped you rather than the others? Your men had twenty-two legs and so had they, Don Camillo, and all legs are equal. Moreover, they are not My business. I am interested in souls. *Da mihi animam, caetera tolle.* I leave the bodies on earth. Don Camillo, where are your brains?'

'I can find them with an effort,' said Don Camillo. 'I was not suggesting that You should have taken charge of my men's legs, which in any case were the best of the lot. But I do say that You did not prevent the dishonesty of one man from giving a foul unjustly against my team.'

'The priest can make a mistake in saying mass, Don Camillo. Why must you deny that others may be mistaken while being in good faith?'

'One can admit of errors in most circumstances, but not when it is a matter of arbitration in sport! When the ball is actually there. . . . Binella is a scoundrel. . . .' He was unable to continue because at that moment the sound of an imploring voice became progressively audible and a man came running into the church, exhausted and gasping, his face convulsed with terror.

'They want to kill me,' he sobbed. 'Save me!'

The crowd had reached the church door and was about to irrupt into the church itself. Don Camillo seized a candlestick weighing half a quintal and brandished it menacingly.

'Back, in God's name, or I strike!' he shouted. 'Remember that anyone who enters here is sacred and immune!'

The crowd hesitated.

'Shame on you, you pack of wolves! Get back to your lairs and pray God to forgive you your savagery.'

The crowd stood in silence, heads were bowed, and there was a general movement of retreat.

'Make the sign of the cross,' Don Camillo ordered them severely, and as he stood there brandishing the candlestick in his huge hand he seemed a very Samson.

Everyone made the sign of the cross.

'Between you and the object of your brutality is now the sign of the cross that each one of you has traced with his own hand. Anybody who dares to violate that sacred barrier is a blasphemer. *Vade retro!*' He himself stood back and closed the church door, drawing the bolt, but there was no need. The fugitive had sunk on to a bench and was still panting. 'Thank you, Don Camillo,' he murmured.

Don Camillo made no immediate reply. He paced to and fro for a few minutes and then pulled up opposite the man. 'Binella!' said Don Camillo in accents of fury. 'Binella, here in my presence and that of God you dare not lie! There was no foul! How much did that reprobate Peppone give you to make you call a foul in a drawn game?'

'Two thousand five hundred lire.'

'M-m-m-m!' roared Don Camillo, thrusting his fist under his victim's nose.

'But then. . .' moaned Binella.

'Get out,' bawled Don Camillo, pointing to the door.

Once more alone, Don Camillo turned towards the Lord. 'Didn't I tell You that the swine had sold himself? Haven't I a right to be enraged?'

'None at all, Don Camillo,' replied the Lord. 'You started it when you offered Binella two thousand lire to do the same thing. When Peppone bid five hundred lire more, Binella accepted the higher bribe.'

Don Camillo spread out his arms. 'Lord,' he said, 'but if we are to look at it that way, then I emerge as the guilty man.'

'Exactly, Don Camillo. When you, a priest, were the first to make the suggestion, he assumed that there was no harm in the matter, and then, quite naturally, he took the more profitable bid.'

Don Camillo bowed his head. 'And do You mean to tell me that if that unhappy wretch should get beaten up by my men it would be my doing?'

'In a certain sense, yes, because you were the first to lead him into temptation. Nevertheless your sin would have been greater if Binella, accepting your offer, had agreed to cheat on behalf of your team. Because then the Dynamos would have done the beating up and you would have been powerless to stop them.'

Don Camillo reflected awhile. 'In fact,' he said, 'it was better that the others should win.'

'Exactly, Don Camillo.'

'Then, Lord,' said Don Camillo, 'I thank You for having allowed me to lose. And if I tell You that I accept the defeat as a punishment for my dishonesty You must believe that I am really penitent. Because to see a team such as mine who might very well—and I am not bragging—play in Division B, a team that, believe me or not, could swallow up and digest a couple of thousand Dynamos in their stride, to see them beaten . . . is enough to break one's heart and cries for vengeance to God!'

'Don Camillo!' the Lord admonished him, smiling.

'You can't possibly understand me,' sighed Don Camillo. 'Sport is a thing apart. Either one cares, or one doesn't. Do I make myself clear?'

'Only too clear, my poor Don Camillo. I understand you so well that. . . . Come now, when are you going to have your revenge?'

Don Camillo leaped to his feet, his heart swelling with delight. 'Six to nothing!' he shouted. 'Six to nought that they never even see the ball! Do you see that confessional?'

He flung his hat into the air, caught it with a neat kick as it came down and drove it like a thunderbolt into the little window of the confessional.

'Goal!' said the Lord, smiling.

Frank O'Connor

FRANK O'CONNOR, which is the pseudonym of Michael O'Donovan, began, rather optimistically, to prepare a collected edition of his works at the age of twelve. But he had to wait another thirty-five years before the first collected edition of his tales was in print.

O'Donovan, who came from a typical Irish family, is largely self-educated. He has worked as librarian, journalist, and translator, learning several languages when he was forcibly interned by the government of the Irish Free State. When quite young he learned to speak Irish, and read all he could find of Gaelic poetry, music, and legend.

He often tours Ireland on a bicycle, and will put stories from other countries into an Irish setting.

Now he is married to an American wife and lives in Brooklyn, New York.

THE MISER

I

HE USED to sit all day, looking out from behind the dirty little windows of his dirty little shop in Main Street; a man with a smooth oval pate and bleared, melancholy-looking, unblinking eyes; a hanging lip with a fag dangling from it, and hanging unshaven chins. It was a face you'd remember; swollen, ponderous, crimson, with a frame of jet-black hair plastered down on either side with bear's grease; and though the hair grew grey and the face turned yellow it seemed to make no difference: because he never changed his position you did not notice the change which came over him from within, and saw him at the end as you had seen him at first, planted there like an oak or a rock. He scarcely stirred even when someone pushed in the old glazed door and stumbled down the steps from the street. The effort seemed to be too much for him; the bleary, bloodshot eyes travelled slowly to some shelf, the arm reached lifelessly out; the coins dropped in the till. Then he shrugged himself and gazed out into the street again. Sometimes he spoke, and it always gave you a shock, for it was as if the statue of O'Connell had descended from its pedestal and inquired in a melancholy bass voice and with old-fashioned politeness for some member of your family. It was a thing held greatly in his favour that he never forgot an old neighbour.

Sometimes the children tormented him, looking in and making faces at him through the glass, so that they distracted him from his vigil, and then he roared at them without stirring. Sometimes they went too far and his face swelled and grew purple; he staggered to the door and bellowed after them in a powerful resonant voice that echoed to the other end of the town. But mostly he stayed there silent and undisturbed, and the dirt and disorder round him grew and greased his hair and clothes, while his face and chin with their Buddha-like gravity were shiny with spilt gravy. His only luxury was the Woodbine that went out between his lips. The cigarettes were on the shelf behind him, and all he had to do was to reach out for them; he didn't need to turn his head.

He was the last of a very good family, the Devereuxs, who had once been big merchants in the town. People remembered his old father driving into town in his own carriage; indeed, they remembered Tom Devereux himself as a bit of a masher, smoking a cigar and wearing a new flower in his buttonhole every day. But then he married beneath him and the match turned out badly. There was a daughter called Joan but she turned out badly too, started a child and went away, God knows where, and now he had no one to look after him but an old soldier called Faxy, a tall, stringy, ravaged-looking man,

toothless and half mad. Faxy had attached himself to Tom
years before as a batman. He boiled the kettle and brought the
old man a cup of tea in the mornings.

'Orders for the day, general!' he would say then, springing
to attention; and Devereux, after a lot of groaning, would fish
out sixpence from under his pillow.

'And what do you think I am going to get for that?' Faxy
would snarl, the smile withering from his puss.

'Oh, indeed,' Devereux would bellow complacently, 'you
can get a very nice bit of black pudding for that.'

'And is it black pudding you're going to drink instead of tea?'

'But when I haven't it, man?' the old man would shout,
turning purple.

'You haven't, I hear!' Faxy would hiss with a wolfish grin,
stepping from one foot to the other like a child short-taken.
'Come on now, can't you? I can't be waiting the whole day
for it. Baksheesh! Baksheesh for the sahib's tiffin!'

'I tell you to go away and not be annoying me,' Devereux
would shout, and that was all the satisfaction Faxy got. It was a
nightmare to Faxy, trying to get money or credit.

'But he have it, man, he have it,' he would hiss, leaning over
the counters, trying to coax more credit out of the shopkeepers.
'Boxes of it he have, man; nailed down and flowing over. He
have two big trunks of it under the bed alone.'

That was the report in town as well; everyone knew that the
Devereuxs always had the tin and that old Tom hadn't lessened
it much, and at one time or other, every shopkeeper had given
him credit, and all ended by refusing it, seeing the old man
in the window, day after day, looking as though he were
immortal.

2

At long last he did have a stroke and had to take to his bed, upstairs in a stinking room with the sagging windowpanes padded and nailed against draughts from the Main Street, and the flowery wallpaper, layer on layer of it, hanging in bangles from the walls, while Faxy looked after the shop and made hay of the Woodbines and whatever else came handy. Not that there was much, only paraffin oil and candles and maybe a few old things like cards of castor-oil bottles that the commercials left on spec. Whenever a customer went out, bang, bang, bang! old Devereux thumped on the floor for Faxy.

'Who was that went out, Faxy?' he would groan. 'I didn't recognize the voice.'

'That was the Sheenan girl from the lane.'

'Did you ask her how her father was?'

'I did not, indeed, ask how her father was. I have something else to think about.'

'You ought to have asked her all the same,' the old man grumbled. 'What did she want?'

'A couple of candles,' hissed Faxy. 'Is there anything else you'd like to know?'

'It wasn't a couple of candles, Donnell. Don't you try and deceive me. I heard every word of it. I distinctly heard her asking for something else as well.'

'A pity the stroke affected your hearing,' snarled Faxy.

'Don't you try and deceive me, I say,' boomed Devereux. 'I have it all checked, Donnell, every ha'p'orth. Mind now what I'm saying!'

Then one morning while Faxy was smoking a cigarette and studying the racing in the previous day's paper, the shop door opened gently and Father Ring came in. Father Ring was a plausible little Kerryman with a sand-coloured face and a shock of red hair. He was always very deprecating, with an excuse-me air, and came in sideways, on tiptoe, wearing a shocked expression—it is only Kerrymen who can do things like that.

'My poor man,' he whispered, leaning over the counter to Faxy. I'm sorry for your trouble. Himself isn't well on you.'

'If he isn't,' snarled Faxy, looking as much like the Stag at Bay as made no difference, 'he's well looked after.'

'I know that, Faxy,' the priest said, nodding. 'I know that well. Still, 'twould be no harm if I had a few words with him. A man like that might go in a flash. . . . Tell me, Faxy,' he whispered with his hand across his lips and his head to one side, 'are his affairs in order?'

'How the hell would I know when the old devil won't even talk about them?' asked Faxy.

'That's bad, Faxy,' said Father Ring gravely. 'That's very bad. That's a great risk you're running, a man like you that must be owed a lot of money. If anything happened him you might be thrown on the road without a ha'penny. Whisper here to me,' he went on, drawing Faxy closer and whispering into his ear the way no one but a Kerryman can do it, without once taking his eyes off Faxy's face. 'If you want to make sure of your rights, you'd better see he has his affairs in order. Leave it to me and I'll do what I can.' Then he nodded and winked, and away with him upstairs, leaving Faxy gaping after him.

He opened the bedroom door a couple of inches, bowed, and smiled in with his best excuse-me-God-help-me expression. The smile was one of the hardest things he had ever had to do, because the smell was something shocking. Then he tiptoed in respectfully, his hand outstretched.

'My poor man!' he whispered. 'My poor fellow! How are you at all? I needn't ask.'

'Poorly, father, poorly,' rumbled Devereux, rolling his lazy bloodshot eyes at him.

'I can see that. I can see you are. Isn't there anything I can do for you?' Father Ring tiptoed back to the door and gave a glance out at the landing. 'I'm surprised that man of yours didn't send for me,' he said reproachfully. 'You don't look very comfortable. Wouldn't you be better off in hospital?'

'I won't tell you a word of a lie, father,' Devereux said candidly. 'I couldn't afford it.'

'No, to be sure, to be sure, 'tis expensive, 'tis, 'tis,' Father Ring agreed feelingly. 'And you have no one to look after you?'

'I have not, father, I'm sorry to say.'

'Oh, my, my, my! At the end of your days! You couldn't get in touch with the daughter, I suppose?'

'No, father, I could not,' Devereux said shortly.

'I'm sorry about that. Wisha, isn't life queer. A great disappointment, that girl, Julia.'

'Joan, father.'

'Joan I mean. To be sure, to be sure, Joan. A great disappointment.'

'She was, father.'

And then, when Devereux had told his little story, Father Ring, bending forward with his hairy hands joined, whispered:

'Tell me, wouldn't it be a good thing if you had a couple of nuns?'

'A couple of what, father?' asked Devereux in astonishment.

'A couple of nuns. From the hospital. They'd look after you properly.'

'Ah, father,' Devereux said indignantly as though the priest had accused him of some nasty mean action, 'sure I have no money for nuns.'

'Well now,' Father Ring said thoughtfully, 'that's a matter you might leave to me. Myself and the nuns are old friends. Sure, that man, that What's-his-name, that fellow you have downstairs—sure, that poor unfortunate could do nothing for you.'

'Only break my heart, father,' Devereux sighed gustily. 'I won't tell you a word of a lie. He have me robbed.'

'Well, leave it to me,' Father Ring said with a wink. 'He might meet his match.'

Downstairs he whispered into Faxy's ear with his hand shading his mouth and his eyes following someone down the street:

'I'd say nothing just at present, Faxy. I'll get a couple of nuns to look after him. You might find him easier to deal with after that.'

3

It wasn't until the following morning that Faxy understood the full implications of that. Then it was too late. The nuns were installed and couldn't be shifted; one old, tough, and hairy, whom Faxy instantly christened 'the sergeant-major', the other young and good-looking.

'Come now,' the sergeant-major said to Faxy. 'Put on this apron and give that floor a good scrubbing.'

'Scrubbing?' bawled Faxy. Name of Ja—' and stopped himself just in time. 'What's wrong with that floor?' he snarled. 'You could eat your dinner off that floor.'

'You'd have the making of it anyway,' the sergeant-major said dryly, 'only 'twouldn't be very appetizing. I have a bath of water on for you. And mind and put plenty of Jeyes' Fluid.'

'I was discharged from the army with rheumatics,' Faxy said, grabbing his knee illustratively. 'Light duty is all I'm fit for. I have it on my discharge papers. And who's going to look after the shop?'

It was all no use. Down he had to go on his knees like any old washerwoman with a coarse apron round his waist and scrub every inch of the floor with carbolic soap and what he called Jeyes's Fluid. The sergeant-major was at his heels the whole time, telling him to change the water and wash the brush and cracking jokes about his rheumatics till she had him leaping. Then, under the eyes of the whole street, he had to get out on the window-ledge, wash the window, and strip away the comforting felt that had kept out generations of draughts; and afterwards scrape the walls while the young nun went after him with a spray, killing the bugs, she said—as if a couple of bugs ever did anyone any harm!

Faxy muttered rebelliously to himself about people who never saw anything of life only to plank their backside on a feather-bed while poor soldiers had to sleep out with nothing but gravestones for mattresses and corpses all round them and never complained. From his Way of the Cross he glared at Devereux, only asking for one word of an order to mutiny, but the old man only looked away at the farther wall with bleared and frightened eyes. He seemed to imagine that all he had to do was lie doggo to make the sergeant-major think he was dead.

But then his own turn came and Faxy, on face and hands on the landing, looked up through the chink in the door and saw them strip Devereux naked to God and the world and wash him all down the belly. 'Sweet Christ preserve us!' he muttered. It looked to him like the end of the world. Then they turned the old man over and washed him all down the back. He never uttered a groan or a moan, and relaxed like a Christian martyr in the flames, looking away with glassy eyes at floor and ceiling so that he would not embarrass them seeing what they had no right to see.

He contained himself till he couldn't contain himself any longer and then burst into a loud wail for Faxy and the bucket,

but Faxy realized to his horror that even this little bit of decency
was being denied him and that he was being made to sit up in
bed with the young one holding him under the armpits while
the sergeant-major planted him on top of some new-fangled
yoke she was after ordering up from the chemist's.

It was too much for Faxy. At heart he was a religious man
and to see women dressed as nuns behaving with no more
modesty than hospital orderlies broke his spirit entirely. He
moaned and tore his hair and cursed his God. He didn't wait
to see the old man's hair cut, and his mattress and bedclothes
that he had lain in so comfortably all the long years taken out
to be burned, but prowled from shop to street and street back
to shop, looking up at the window or listening at the foot of the
stairs, telling his sad tale to all who passed. 'We didn't know
how happy we were,' he snarled. 'God pity the poor that fall
into their hands! We had a king's life and look at us now, like
paupers in the workhouse without a thing we can call our
own!'

He was even afraid to go into his own kitchen for fear the
sergeant-major would fall on him and strip him as well. The
woman had no notion of modesty. She might even say he was
dirty. A woman who'd say what she had said about the bedroom floor would stop at nothing. It was only when her back
was turned that he crept up the stairs on tiptoe and silently
pushed in the bedroom door. The change from the morning
was terrible. It went to Faxy's heart. He knew now he no longer
had a home to call his own; windows open above and below,
a draught that would skin a brass monkey and flowers in a
vase on a table near the bed. The old man was lying there like
a corpse, clean, comfortable, and collapsed. It was only after a
few moments that he opened his weary bloodshot eyes and
gazed at Faxy with a far-away, heartbroken air. Faxy glared
down at him like a great gaunt bird of prey, clutching his

ragged old shirt back from his chest and shaking his skeleton head.

'Jasus!' he whispered in agony. ''Tis like a second crucifixion.'

'Would you gimme a fag, Faxy, if you please?' pleaded Devereux in a dying voice.

'Ask your old jenny-asses for one!' hissed Faxy malevolently.

4

Devereux was just beginning to get over the shock when Father Ring called again. Whatever it might have cost himself and Faxy, the clean-up was a great ease to Father Ring.

'My poor man!' he said, shaking Devereux's hand and casting a sly glance round the room, 'how are you today? You're looking better. Well, now, aren't they great little women? Tell me, are they feeding you properly?'

'Very nice, father,' Devereux said feebly in a tone of astonishment, as if he thought after the shocking way they had already behaved to him, starvation was the only thing he could have expected. 'Very nice indeed. I had a nice little bit of chicken and a couple of poppies and a bit of cabbage.'

'Sure, you couldn't have nicer,' said Father Ring, smacking his own lips over it.

'I had, indeed,' Devereux boomed, raising his arm and looking at the clean hairy skin inside the shirtband as though he wondered whom it belonged to. 'And I had rice pudding,' he added reflectively, 'and a cup of tea.'

'Ah, man, they'll have you trotting like a circus pony before they're done with you,' said Father Ring.

'I'm afraid it come too late, father,' sighed the old man as if the same notion had crossed his mind. 'I had a lot of hardship.'

'You had, you poor soul, you had,' sighed Father Ring.

'And, of course, when it comes to our turn we must be resigned. I say we must be resigned,' he added firmly. 'It comes to us all, sooner or later, and if our conscience is clear and our—oh, by the way, I nearly forgot it; my head is going—I suppose your own little affairs are in order?'

'What's that you say, father?'. Devereux whispered with a timid, trapped air, raising his head from the pillow.

'Your affairs,' murmured Father Ring. 'Are they in order? I mean, have you your will made?'

'I won't tell you a word of a lie, father,' the old man said bashfully. 'I have not.'

'Well, now, listen to me,' Father Ring said persuasively, pulling his chair closer to the bed, 'wouldn't it be a good thing for you to do? 'Tisn't, God knows, for the little that either of us will leave, but for the sake of peace and quietness after we've gone. You saw them as I did myself, fighting over a few sticks.'

'I did, father, I did.'

''Tis the scandal of it,' said Father Ring. 'And God between us and all harm, the hour might come for any of us. It might come for myself and I a younger man than you.'

'Wouldn't I want an attorney, father?' Devereux asked timidly.

'Ah, what attorney?' exclaimed Father Ring. 'Aren't I better than any attorney? 'Pon my soul, I don't know why I didn't go in for the law. As it happens,' he added, scowling and fumbling in his pockets, 'I have some writing paper with me. I hope I didn't leave my specs behind. I did! As sure as you're there, I did. What sort of old head have I . . .? No, I declare to my goodness, I brought them for once. Ah, man alive,' he exclaimed, looking at Devereux over the specs, 'I have to do this every month of my life. 'Tis astonishing, the number of people that put it on the long finger. . . . I may as well get it down as I'm here. I can write the rigmarole in after. . . . What'll we say to begin with? You'd like to leave a couple of pounds for Masses, I suppose?'

'God knows I would, father,' Devereux said devoutly.

'Well, what'll we say? Give me a figure! Ten? Twenty?'

'I suppose so, father,' Devereux replied hesitatingly.

'Well, now, make it whatever you like,' said Father Ring, pointing the fountain pen like a dart at him and giving him a long look through the spectacles, a sort of professional look, quite different from the ones he gave over and round them. 'But, remember, Masses are the only investment you can draw on in the next world. The only friends you can be sure won't forget you. Think again before you say the last word on Masses.'

'How much would you say yourself, father?' asked Devereux, hypnotized by the gleam of the spectacles like a rabbit by the headlights of a car.

'Well, that's a matter for you. You know what you can afford. You might like to make it a hundred. Or even more.'

'We'll say a hundred so,' said Devereux.

'Good man! Good man! I like a man that knows his own mind. You'd be astonished, the people that don't seem to be able to say "yes" or "no". And what'll we do about the—' he nodded towards the door—'the holy ladies? 'Twould be expected.'

'Would the same thing be enough, father?'

'To tell you the truth, Mr. Devereux, I think it would,' said Father Ring, bobbing his head and giving Devereux an unprofessional dart over the top of his spectacles. 'I'll go farther. I'd say 'twould be generous. Women are lick alike. I don't know how it is, Mr. Devereux, but a woman crossed in love finds some fatal attraction in building. Building is the ruin of those poor women. A fool and his money—but you know the old proverb.'

'I do, father.'

'And the monks? As we're on the subject of charities, what are we going to do about the monks?'

Devereux gave him an appealing glance. Father Ring rose, pursing his lips and putting his hands behind his back. He stood at the window and gazed down the street, his head on his chest and his eyes strained over his glasses.

'Look at that scut, Foley, sneaking into Johnny Desmond's,' he said as though to himself, 'That fellow will be the death of his poor unfortunate wife. . . . I think so, Mr. Devereux,' he added in a loud voice, turning on his heel and raising his head like a man who has received a sudden illumination. 'I think so. Religious orders! 'Tisn't for me to be criticizing them, God knows, but they'd surprise you. 'Pon my soul, they'd surprise you! The jealousy between them over a miserable couple of hundred pounds! Those poor fellows would be fretting over a slight like that for years to come.'

''Twouldn't be wishing to me,' said Devereux, shaking his head regretfully.

''Twouldn't, man, 'twouldn't, 'twouldn't,' cried Father Ring as if astonished at Devereux's perspicacity, and implying by his tone that if the bad wishes of the monks didn't actually follow the old man to the next world they'd make very heavy weather for any prayers which did. 'You're right, Mr. Devereux, it would not be wishing to you. . . . Now, coming nearer home,' he whispered with a nervous glance over his shoulder, 'what about that man of yours? They'll be expecting you to provide for him.'

'He robbed me, father,' Devereux said sullenly, his heavy face settling into the expression of an obstinate child.

'Ah, let me alone, let me alone!' said Father Ring, waving the paper in his face with exasperation. 'I know all about it. That British Army! 'Tis the ruination of thousands.'

'The couple of cigarettes I'd have,' the old man went on, turning his red eyes on the priest while his deep voice throbbed like a 'cello with the dint of self-pity, 'he'd steal them on me. Often and often—I won't tell you a word of a lie, father—I'd go down to the shop of a morning and I wouldn't have a smoke. Not a smoke!'

'Oh, my, my!' said Father Ring, clucking and nodding over the villainy of man.

'The packets of Lux,' intoned Devereux solemnly, raising his right hand in affirmation, 'that's as true as the Almighty God is looking down on me this moment, father, he'd take them and sell them from door to door, a half dozen for the price of a medium. And I sitting here, gasping for a cigarette!'

'Well, well!' sighed the priest. 'But still, Mr. Devereux, you know you're after forgiving him all that.'

'Forgiving him is one thing,' the old man said stubbornly, 'but leaving him a legacy is another thing entirely, father. Oh, no.'

'But as a sign that you forgive him!' the priest said coaxingly. 'A—what'll I call it?—a token! Some little thing.'

'Not a ha'penny, father,' said Devereux in the voice of a judge with the black cap on. 'Not one solitary ha'penny.'

'Well, now, Mr. Devereux,' Father Ring pleaded, 'fifty pounds. What is it? 'Tis neither here not there and 'twould mean a lot to that poor wretch.'

Suddenly the door burst open and Faxy, who had been listening at the keyhole, charged in on them, a great, gaunt skeleton of a man with mad eyes and clenched fists.

'Fifty pounds?' he shouted. 'Fifty pounds? Is it mad ye are, the pair of ye?'

Old Devereux began to struggle frantically up in the bed, throwing off the clothes with his swollen old hands and gasping for breath so that he could tell Faxy what he thought of him.

'You robber!' he croaked away back in his throat. 'If I done you justice I'd have you up in the body of the jail.'

'Come now, Mr. Devereux, come, come!' cried Father Ring, alarmed that the old man might drop dead on him before the will was even sketched. 'Compose yourself,' he said, putting down his papers and trying to get Devereux to lie back.

'I won't give him a ha'penny,' roared Devereux in a voice that could be heard at the opposite side of the street. 'Not one ha'penny! Leave him support himself out of all he stole from the till!'

'And a hell of a lot there ever was to steal!' hissed Faxy with his gaunt head bowed, grinning back at him.

'Not a ha'penny!' repeated the old man frantically, pummelling his knees with his fists and blowing himself up like a balloon till he turned all colours.

'Two hundred and fifty pounds,' snarled Faxy with his toothless gums, pointing at the palm of his left hand as if he had it all noted there. 'That's what I'm owed. I have it all down in black and white. Back wages. The War Office won't see me wronged.'

'You robber!' panted Devereux.

'Sister!' cried Father Ring, throwing the door open. 'Sister Whatever-your-name-is, send for the police! Tell them I want this fellow locked up.'

'Leave that one out of it!' hissed Faxy, dragging Father Ring back from the door. Faxy wasn't afraid of the police, but he was scared out of his wits by the sergeant-major of the nuns. 'We want no women in it. Play fair and fight like a man. Fair play is all I ask. I done for him what no one else would do.'

'Mr. Devereux,' Father Ring said earnestly, 'he's right. The man is right. He's entitled to something. He could upset the will.'

'God knows, father, that's not what I want,' said Faxy. He

sat on the edge of the bed, began to sob, and brushed away the tears with his hand. 'I deserved better after my years of hardship. No one knows what I went through with him.'

'You sweet God, listen to him!' croaked Devereux despairingly. 'Black puddings and old sausages. Not one decent bite of food crossed my lips, father, all the long years he's with me. Not till the blessed nuns came.'

'Because they can get the credit,' snarled Faxy, shaking his fist at his boss while his tears dried as though by magic. 'If you handed me out the money instead of locking it up, you could have bacon and cabbage every day of the week. I was batman to better men than you. You were too near, and now 'tis going on you whether you like it or not on medicines and Jeyes's Fluid and chamberpots. That's all you have out of it at the end of your days.'

'Be quiet now, be quiet!' said Father Ring. 'You'll get something, even though you don't deserve it. I'll take it on myself to put him down for another hundred, Mr. Devereux. You won't deny me that?'

'A hundred strokes of the cat-and-nine-tails,' grumbled the old man. 'But I won't deny you, father, I'll offer it up. . . . That it might choke you!' he added charitably to Faxy.

'And now, Mr. D., I won't keep you much longer. There's just Julia.'

'Joan, father.'

'Joan, I mean. To be sure, Joan. Or the little—you know who I'm talking of. Was it a little boy? 'Pon my soul, my memory is gone.'

'Nothing, father,' Devereux said firmly, settling himself back in his pillows and gazing out the window.

'What's that?' Faxy shouted, scandalized. 'Your daughter!'

'This has nothing to do with you, Donnell,' said Devereux. 'It have nothing to do with anyone.'

'Now, you're wrong there, Mr. Devereux,' Father Ring said with a quelling professional glance. 'I say you're wrong there. Whatever little disagreement ye might have or whatever upset she might cause you, this is no time to remember it.'

'I won't leave her a ha'penny, father,' Devereux said firmly. ''Tis no use to be at me. Anything that's over can go to the Church.'

'Christ look down on the poor!' cried Faxy, raising his arms to heaven. 'Stick and stone instead of flesh and bone.'

'Will you be quiet?' snapped Father Ring. 'Now, Mr. Devereux, I understand your feelings; I understand them perfectly, but 'tisn't right. Do you know what they'd say? Have you any notion of the wickedness of people in this town? They'd say there was undue influence, Mr. Devereux. You might have the whole will upset on you for the sake of— what'll I say? A hundred? Two hundred? A trifle anyway.'

'This is my will, father, not yours,' Devereux said with sudden, surprising dignity. 'I'm after telling you my wishes, and Donnell here is a witness. Everything else is to go to the Church, barring a few pounds to keep the family vault in order. The Devereuxs are an old family, father,' he added with calm pride. 'They were a great family in their day, and I'd like the grave to be respected when I'm gone.'

That night the will was signed and the substance of it was the talk of the town. Many blamed old Devereux for being hard and unnatural; more blamed Father Ring for being so grasping. Faxy got credit on the strength of it and came home fighting drunk, under the impression that the old man was already dead and that the priest had cheated him out of his inheritance; but the nuns locked him out and he slept in the straw in Kearney's yard, waking in the middle of the night and howling like a dog for his lost master.

But Devereux had no intention of dying. He began to

improve visibly under the nuns' care. He had a little handbell on the table by his bed, and whenever he felt bored he rang for the sergeant-major to keep him company. He had taken a great fancy to her, and he just rang whenever he remembered anything more about the history of the Devereuxs. When he tired of this he held her hand while she read him a chapter from *The Imitation of Christ* or *The Lives of the Saints*.

'That's beautiful reading, Sister,' he said, stroking her hand.

'Sure, there's nothing like it,' said the sergeant-major.

'Beautiful reading,' sighed Devereux with a far-away air. 'Don't we miss a lot in life, sister?'

'Ah, musha, we all miss a lot, but God will make it up to us, we hope. Sunshine in this life, shadow in the next.'

'I'd like a bit of sunshine too, sister,' he said. 'Ye're very good to me and I didn't forget ye in my will.'

He talked a lot about his will and even said he was thinking of changing it in favour of the nuns. The only trouble was that Father Ring wouldn't approve, being a strong-minded man himself, and Devereux could never warm to solicitors from the time they started sending him letters. The rudeness of some of those solicitors' letters was still on his mind. He got really lively at times and even suggested that the sergeant-major might read him some novels by Mrs. Braddon. He was very fond of the works of Mrs. Braddon, he said.

'I suppose you'll be renewing that bottle for me, sister?' he said on one occasion. 'I wonder would you get me something else at the same time?'

'I will to be sure, Mr. Devereux. What is it?'

'Well,' he said bashfully, 'I'd like a little drop of hair-oil, if you please. My hair doesn't lie down well without it. The scented kind is the kind I like.'

She got him the hair-oil and did his hair for him while he looked at her fondly and commented on her hands. Beautiful,

gentle hands she had, he said. Then she gave him the mirror
to see himself, and he was so shocked that tears came to his
eyes.

'Now,' she said briskly, 'there's a fine handsome man for
you!'

'I was very handsome once, sister,' he said mournfully. 'The
handsomest man in the town, I was supposed to be. People used
to stop and look after me in the street. Dandy Devereux they
used to call me.'

Then he asked for the scissors to clip his moustache.

He made a most beautiful and edifying death, with the nuns
at either side of him saying the prayers for the dying, and when
they had laid him out the sergeant-major went down to the
kitchen and had a good cry to herself.

''Tis a hard old life,' she said to the young nun. 'You're left
with them long enough to get fond of them, and then either
they get better or they die on you, and you never see them
again. If 'twas only an old dog you'd be sorry for him, and he
was a fine gentlemanly old man, God rest him.'

Then, having tidied away her pots and pans and had a
last look at old Tom Devereux, the man who had stroked
her hands and praised them as no one else had done since
she was a girl, she washed her eyes and went back to her
convent.

After Requiem High Mass next day Devereux went to join
the rest of his family within the ruined walls of the abbey they
had founded in the fifteenth century, and by the time Father
Ring got back from the funeral Faxy had already started prying.
The great iron-bound chests were in the centre of the floor
and Faxy had borrowed a set of tools. They opened the chests
between them, but there was nothing inside only old screws,
bolts, washers, bits of broken vases and an enormous selection
of pipe-bowls and stems. Father Ring was so incredulous that

he put on his glasses to examine them better. By that time he was ready to believe they were pieces of eight in disguise.

'I made a great mistake,' he said, sitting back on the floor beside the chest. 'I should have asked him where he had it.'

He still had not even faced the possibility that Devereux hadn't it. They stayed on till midnight, searching. Next day they had two men from the builders in. Every floor was ripped up, every chimney searched, every hollow bit of wall burst in. Faxy was first everywhere with a lighted candle, and Father Ring followed, stroking his chin. A crowd had gathered in the street, and at intervals the priest stood at the window and surveyed them moodily over his glasses. He had a nasty feeling that the crowd would be well pleased if he failed.

Eddie Murphy, the undertaker, came up the stairs looking anxious. Eddie was owed thirty quid so he had good cause for anxiety.

'Did ye find it, father?' he asked.

'I'm afraid, Eddie,' Father Ring said, looking round his glasses, 'we were had. We were had, boy, all of us. 'Tis a great disappointment, a great disappointment, Eddie, but 'pon my soul, he was a remarkable man.'

Then he took his shabby old soft hat and went home.

Evelyn Waugh

EVELYN WAUGH comes from a family of writers. His father was a writer, publisher, and literary critic, and his brother Alec is a popular novelist.

Waugh wrote his first novel when he was only twenty-two. In the years which followed he travelled extensively in Europe, Africa, and America. During the war he was commissioned in the Royal Marines, and later transferred to the Royal Horse Guards.

When he was a young man, he was received into the Roman Catholic Church, and he is today one of our leading Catholic writers.

Since 1937 he and his wife and six children have lived in Gloucestershire.

TACTICAL EXERCISE

JOHN VERNEY married Elizabeth in 1938, but it was not until the winter of 1945 that he came to hate her steadily and fiercely. There had been countless brief gusts of hate before this, for it was a thing which came easily to him. He was not what is normally described as a bad-tempered man, rather the reverse; a look of fatigue and abstraction was the only visible sign of the passion which possessed him, as others are possessed by laughter or desire, several times a day.

During the war he passed among those he served with as a phlegmatic fellow. He did not have his good or his bad days; they were all uniformly good or bad; good in that he did what had to be done, expeditiously without ever 'getting in a flap' or 'going off the deep end'; bad from the intermittent, invisible sheet-lightning of hate which flashed and flickered deep inside him at every obstruction or reverse. In his orderly room, when, as a company commander, he faced the morning procession of defaulters and malingerers; in the mess when the subalterns disturbed his reading by playing the wireless; at the Staff College when the 'syndicate' disagreed with his solution; at Brigade H.Q. when the staff-sergeant mislaid a file or the telephone orderly muddled a call; when the driver of his car missed a turning; later, in hospital, when the doctor seemed to look cursorily at his wound and the nurses stood gossiping jauntily at the beds of more likeable patients instead of doing their duty to him—in all the annoyances of army life which others dismissed with an oath and a shrug, John Verney's eyelids drooped wearily, a tiny grenade of hate exploded, and the fragments rang and ricocheted round the steel walls of his mind.

There had been less to annoy him before the war. He had some money and the hope of a career in politics. Before marriage he served his apprenticeship to the Liberal party in two hopeless by-elections. The Central Office then rewarded him with a constituency in outer London which offered a fair chance in the next general election. In the eighteen months before the war he nursed this constituency from his flat in Belgravia and travelled frequently on the Continent to study political conditions. These studies convinced him that war was inevitable; he denounced the Munich agreement pungently and secured a commission in the Territorial Army.

Into the peacetime life Elizabeth fitted unobtrusively. She was his cousin. In 1938 she had reached the age of twenty-six, four years his junior, without falling in love. She was a calm, handsome young woman, an only child, with some money of her own and more to come. As a girl, in her first season, an injudicious remark, let slip and overheard, got her the reputation of cleverness. Those who knew her best ruthlessly called her 'deep'.

Thus condemned to social failure, she languished in the ballrooms of Pont Street for another year and then settled down to a life of concert-going and shopping with her mother, until she surprised her small circle of friends by marrying John Verney. Courtship and consummation were tepid, cousinly, harmonious. They agreed, in face of coming war, to remain childless. No one knew what Elizabeth felt or thought about anything. Her judgments were mainly negative, deep or dull as you cared to take them. She had none of the appearance of a woman likely to inflame great hate.

John Verney was discharged from the Army early in 1945 with a M.C. and one leg, for the future, two inches shorter than the other. He found Elizabeth living in Hampstead with her parents, his uncle and aunt. She had kept him informed of the changes in her condition, but, preoccupied, he had not clearly imagined them. Their flat had been requisitioned by a government office; their furniture and books sent to a repository and totally lost, partly burned by a bomb, partly pillaged by firemen. Elizabeth, who was a linguist, had gone to work in a clandestine branch of the Foreign Office.

Her parents' house had once been a substantial Georgian villa overlooking the Heath. John Verney arrived there early in the morning after a crowded night's journey from Liverpool. The wrought-iron railings and gates had been rudely torn away by the salvage collectors, and in the front garden, once so neat, weeds and shrubs grew in a rank jungle trampled at night by courting soldiers. The back garden was a single, small bomb-crater; heaped clay, statuary, and the bricks and glass of ruined greenhouses; dry stalks of willow-herb stood breast high over the mounds. All the windows were gone from the back of the house, replaced by shutters of card and board, which put the main rooms in perpetual darkness. 'Welcome to Chaos and Old Night,' said his uncle genially.

There were no servants; the old had fled, the young had been conscripted for service. Elizabeth made him some tea before leaving for her office.

Here he lived, lucky, Elizabeth told him, to have a home. Furniture was unprocurable, furnished flats commanded a price beyond their income, which was now taxed to a bare wage. They might have found something in the country, but Elizabeth, being childless, could not get release from her work. Moreover, he had his constituency.

This, too, was transformed. A factory wired round like a prisoner-of-war camp stood in the public gardens. The streets surrounding it, once the trim houses of potential Liberals, had been bombed, patched, confiscated, and filled with an immigrant proletarian population. Every day he received a heap of complaining letters from constituents exiled in provincial boarding-houses. He had hoped that his decoration and his limp might earn him sympathy, but he found the new inhabitants indifferent to the fortunes of war. Instead they showed a sceptical curiosity about Social Security. 'They're nothing but a lot of reds,' said the Liberal agent.

'You mean I shan't get in?'

'Well, we'll give them a good fight. The Tories are putting up a Battle-of-Britain pilot. I'm afraid he'll get most of what's left of the middle-class vote.'

In the event John Verney came bottom of the poll, badly. A rancorous Jewish schoolteacher was elected. The Central Office paid his deposit, but the election had cost him dear. And when it was over there was absolutely nothing for John Verney to do.

He remained in Hampstead, helped his aunt make the beds after Elizabeth had gone to her office, limped to the greengrocer and fishmonger, and stood full of hate in the queues; he helped Elizabeth wash up at night. They ate in the kitchen, where his aunt cooked deliciously the scanty rations. Hisuncle went three days a week to help pack parcels for Java.

Elizabeth, the deep one, never spoke of her work, which, in fact, was concerned with setting up hostile and oppressive governments in Eastern Europe. One evening at a restaurant, a man came and spoke to her, a tall young man whose sallow aquiline face was full of intellect and humour. 'That's the head of my department,' she said. 'He's so amusing.'

'Looks like a Jew.'

'I believe he is. He's a strong Conservative and hates the work,' she added hastily, for since his defeat in the election John had become fiercely anti-Semitic.

'There is absolutely no need to work for the State now,' he said. 'The war's over.'

'Our work is just beginning. They won't let any of us go. You must understand what conditions are in this country.'

It often fell to Elizabeth to explain 'conditions' to him. Strand by strand, knot by knot, through the coalless winter, she exposed the vast net of governmental control which had been woven in his absence. He had been reared in traditional Liberalism and the system revolted him. More than this, it had him caught, personally, tripped up, tied, tangled; wherever he wanted to go, whatever he wanted to do or have done, he found himself baffled and frustrated. And as Elizabeth explained she found herself defending. This regulation was necessary to avoid that ill; such a country was suffering, as Britain was not, for having neglected such a precaution; and so on, calmly and reasonably.

'I know it's maddening John, but you must realize it's the same for everyone.'

'That's what all you bureaucrats want,' he said. 'Equality through slavery. The two-class state—proletarians and officials.'

Elizabeth was part and parcel of it. She worked for the State and the Jews. She was a collaborator with the new, alien, occupying power. And as the winter wore on and the gas burned feebly in the stove, and the rain blew in through the patched windows, as at length spring came and buds broke in the obscene wilderness round the house, Elizabeth in his mind became something more important. She became a symbol. For just as soldiers in far-distant camps think of their wives, with a tenderness they seldom felt at home, as the embodiment of all the good things they have left behind, wives who perhaps were scolds and drabs, but in the desert and jungle became transfigured until their trite air-letters become texts of hope, so Elizabeth grew in John Verney's despairing mind to more than human malevolence as the archpriestess and maenad of the century of the common man.

'You aren't looking well, John,' said his aunt. 'You and Elizabeth ought to get away for a bit. She is due for leave at Easter.'

'The State is granting her a supplementary ration of her husband's company, you mean. Are we sure she has filled in all the correct forms? Or are commissars of her rank above such things?'

Uncle and aunt laughed uneasily. John made his little jokes with such an air of weariness, with such a droop of the eyelids that they sometimes struck chill in that family circle. Elizabeth regarded him gravely and silently.

John was far from well. His leg was in constant pain so that he no longer stood in queues. He slept badly; as also, for the first time in her life, did Elizabeth. They shared a room now, for the winter rains had brought down ceilings in many parts of the shaken house and the upper rooms were thought to be

unsafe. They had twin beds on the ground floor in what had
once been her father's library. They lay night after night six
feet apart in the darkness. Once when John had been awake for
two hours he turned on the lamp that stood on the table
between them. Elizabeth was lying with her eyes wide open
staring at the ceiling.

'I'm sorry. Did I wake you?'

'I haven't been asleep.'

'I thought I'd read for a bit. Will it disturb you?'

'Not at all.'

She turned away. John read for an hour. He did not know
whether she was awake or asleep when he turned off the light.

Often after that he longed to put on the light, but was afraid
to find her awake and staring. Instead, he lay, as others lie in a
luxurious rapture of love, hating her.

It did not occur to him to leave her; or, rather, it did occur
from time to time, but he hopelessly dismissed the thought.
Her life was bound tight to his; her family was his family; their
finances were intertangled and their expectations lay together
in the same quarters. To leave her would be to start fresh, alone
and naked in a strange world; and lame and weary at the age of
thirty-eight, John Verney had not the heart to move.

He loved no one else. He had nowhere to go, nothing to do.
Moreover he suspected, of late, that it would not hurt her if
he went. And, above all, the single steadfast desire left to him
was to do her ill. 'I wish she were dead,' he said to himself as
he lay awake at night. 'I wish she were dead.'

Sometimes they went out together. As the winter passed,
John took to dining once or twice a week at his club. He
assumed that on these occasions she stayed at home, but one
morning it transpired that she too had dined out the evening
before. He did not ask with whom, but his aunt did, and
Elizabeth replied, 'Just someone from the office.'

'The Jew?' John asked.

'As a matter of fact, it was.'

'I hope you enjoyed it.'

'Quite. A beastly dinner, of course, but he's very amusing.'

One night when he returned from his club, after a dismal little dinner and two crowded Tube journeys, he found Elizabeth in bed and deeply asleep. She did not stir when he entered. Unlike her normal habit, she was snoring. He stood for a minute, fascinated by this new and unlovely aspect of her, her head thrown back, her mouth open and slightly dribbling at the corner. Then he shook her. She muttered something, turned over, and slept heavily and soundlessly.

Half an hour later, as he was striving to compose himself for sleep, she began to snore again. He turned on the light, and looked at her more closely and noticed with surprise, which suddenly changed to joyous hope, that there was a tube of unfamiliar pills, half empty, beside her on the bed table.

He examined it. '24 Comprimés narcotiques, hypnotiques,' he read, and then in large scarlet letters, 'NE PAS DÉPASSER DEUX.' He counted those which were left. Eleven.

With tremulous butterfly wings hope began to flutter in his heart, became a certainty. He felt a fire kindle and spread inside him until he was deliciously suffused in every limb and organ. He lay, listening to the snores, with the pure excitement of a child on Christmas Eve. 'I shall wake up tomorrow and find her dead,' he told himself, as once he had felt the flaccid stocking at the foot of his bed and told himself, 'Tomorrow I shall wake up and find it full.' Like a child, he longed to sleep to hasten the morning and, like a child, he was wildly ecstatically sleepless. Presently he swallowed two of the pills himself and almost at once was unconscious.

Elizabeth always rose first to make breakfast for the family. She was at the dressing-table when sharply, without drowsiness, his memory stereoscopically clear about the incidents of the night before, John awoke. 'You've been snoring,' she said.

Disappointment was so intense that at first he could not speak. Then he said, 'You snored, too, last night.'

'It must be the sleeping-tablet I took. I must say it gave me a good night.'

'Only one?'

'Yes, two's the most that's safe.'

'Where did you get them?'

'A friend at the office—the one you called the Jew. He has them prescribed by a doctor for when he's working too hard. I told him I wasn't sleeping, so he gave me half a bottle.'

'Could he get me some?'

'I expect so. He can do most things like that.'

So he and Elizabeth began to drug themselves regularly and passed long, vacuous nights. But often John delayed, letting the beatific pill lie beside his glass of water, while knowing the vigil was terminable at will, he postponed the joy of unconsciousness, heard Elizabeth's snores, and hated her sumptuously.

One evening while the plans for the holidays were still under discussion, John and Elizabeth went to the cinema. The film was a murder story of no great ingenuity but with showy scenery. A bride murdered her husband by throwing him out of a window, down a cliff. Things were made easy for her by his taking a lonely lighthouse for their honeymoon. He was very rich and she wanted his money. All she had to do was to confide in the local doctor and a few neighbours that her husband frightened her by walking in his sleep; she doped his coffee, dragged him from the bed to the balcony—a feat of some strength—where she had already broken away a yard of balustrade, and rolled him over. Then she went back to bed, gave the alarm the next morning, and wept over the mangled body which was presently discovered half awash on the rocks.

Retribution overtook her later, but at the time the thing was a complete success.

'I wish it were as easy as that,' thought John, and in a few hours the whole tale had floated away in those lightless attics of the mind where films and dreams and funny stories lie spider-shrouded for a lifetime unless, as sometimes happens, an intruder brings them to light.

Such a thing happened a few weeks later when John and Elizabeth went for their holiday. Elizabeth found the place.

It belonged to someone in her office. It was named Good Hope Fort, and stood on the Cornish coast. 'It's only just been derequisitioned,' she said; 'I expect we shall find it in pretty bad condition.'

'We're used to that,' said John. It did not occur to him that she should spend her leave anywhere but with him. She was as much part of him as his maimed and aching leg.

They arrived on a gusty April afternoon after a train journey of normal discomfort. A taxi drove them eight miles from the station, through deep Cornish lanes, past granite cottages and disused, archaic tin-workings. They reached the village which gave the houses its postal address, passed through it and out along a track which suddenly emerged from its high banks into open grazing land on the cliff's edge, high, swift clouds and sea-birds wheeling overhead, the turf at their feet alive with fluttering wild flowers, salt in the air, below them the roar of the Atlantic breaking on the rocks, a middle-distance of indigo and white tumbled waters and beyond it the serene arc of the horizon. Here was the house.

'Your father,' said John, 'would now say, "Your castle hath a pleasant seat".'

'Well, it has rather, hasn't it?'

It was a small stone building on the very edge of the cliff, built a century or so ago for defensive purposes, converted to a private house in the years of peace, taken again by the Navy during the war as a signal station, now once more reverting to gentler uses. Some coils of rusty wire, a mast, the concrete foundations of a hut, gave evidence of its former masters.

'A woman comes up every morning from the village. I said we shouldn't want her this evening. I see she's left us some oil for the lamps. She's got a fire going too, bless her, and plenty of wood. Oh, and look what I've got as a present from father. I promised not to tell you until we arrived. A bottle of whisky. Wasn't it sweet of him. He's been hoarding his ration for three months . . .! Elizabeth talked brightly as she began to arrange the luggage. 'There's a room for each of us. This is the only proper living-room, but there's a study in case you feel like doing any work. I believe we shall be quite comfortable. . . .'

The living-room was built with two stout bays, each with a French window opening on a balcony which over-hung the sea. John opened one and the sea-wind filled the room. He stepped out, breathed deeply, and then said suddenly: 'Hullo, this is dangerous.'

At one place, between the windows, the cast-iron balustrade had broken away and the stone ledge lay open over the cliff. He looked at the gap and at the foaming rocks below, momentarily puzzled. The irregular polyhedron of memory rolled uncertainly and came to rest.

He had been here before, a few weeks ago, on the gallery of the lighthouse in that swiftly forgotten film. He stood there looking down. It was exactly thus that the waves had come swirling over the rocks, had broken and dropped back with the spray falling about them. This was the sound they had made; this was the broken ironwork and the sheer edge.

Elizabeth was still talking in the room, her voice drowned by the wind and sea. John returned to the room, shut and fastened the door. In the quiet she was saying '. . . only got the furniture out of store last week. He left the woman from the village to arrange it. She's got some queer ideas, I must say. Just look where she put. . . .'

'What did you say this house was called?'

'Good Hope.'

'A good name.'

That evening John drank a glass of his father-in-law's whisky, smoked a pipe, and planned. He had been a good tactician. He made a leisurely, mental 'appreciation of the situation'. Object: murder.

When they rose to go to bed he asked: 'You packed the tablets?'

'Yes, a new tube. But I am sure I shan't want any tonight.'

'Neither shall I,' said John, 'the air is wonderful.'

During the following days he considered the tactical problem. It was entirely simple. He had the 'staff-solution' already. He considered it in the words and form he had used in the Army. . . . 'Courses open to the enemy . . . achievement of surprise . . . consolidation of success.' The staff-solution was exemplary. At the beginning of the first week, he began to put it into execution.

Already, by easy stages, he had made himself known in the village. Elizabeth was a friend of the owner; he the returned hero, still a little strange in civvy street. 'The first holiday my wife and I have had together for six years,' he told them in the golf club and, growing more confidential at the bar, hinted that they were thinking of making up for lost time and starting a family.

On another evening he spoke of war-strain, of how in this war the civilians had had a worse time of it than the services. His wife, for instance; stuck it all through the blitz; office work all day, bombs at night. She ought to get right away, alone somewhere for a long stretch; her nerves had suffered; nothing serious, but to tell the truth he wasn't quite happy about it. As a matter of fact he found her walking in her sleep once or twice in London.

His companions knew of similar cases; nothing to worry about, but it wanted watching; didn't want it to develop into anything worse. Had she seen a doctor?

Not yet, John said. In fact she didn't know she had been sleep-walking. He had got her back to bed without waking her. He hoped the sea air would do her good. In fact, she seemed much better already. If she showed any more signs of the trouble when they got home, he knew a very good man to take her to.

The golf club was full of sympathy. John asked if there were a good doctor in the neighbourhood. Yes, they said, old Mackenzie in the village, a first-class man, wasted in a little place like this; not at all stick-in-the-mud. Read the latest books, psychology and all that. They couldn't think why Old Mack had never specialized and made a name for himself.

'I think I might go and talk to Old Mack about it,' said John.

'Do. You couldn't find a better fellow.'

Elizabeth had a fortnight's leave. There were still three days to go when John went off to the village to consult Dr. Mackenzie. He found a grey-haired, genial bachelor in a consulting room that was more like a lawyer's office than a physician's, book-lined, dark, permeated by tobacco smoke.

Seated in the shabby leather armchair he developed in more precise language the story he had told in the golf club. Dr. Mackenzie listened without comment.

'It's the first time I've run against anything like this,' he concluded.

At length Dr. Mackenzie said: 'You got pretty badly knocked about in the war, Mr. Verney?'

'My knee. It still gives me trouble.'

'Bad time in hospital?'

'Three months. A beastly place outside Rome.'

'There's always a good deal of nervous shock in an injury of that kind. It often persists when the wound is healed.'

'Yes, but I don't quite understand . . .!'

'My dear Mr. Verney, your wife asked me to say nothing about it, but I think I must tell you that she has already been here to consult me on this matter.'

'About her sleep-walking? But she can't. . . .' Then John stopped.

'My dear fellow, I quite understand. She thought you didn't know. Twice lately you've been out of bed and she had to lead you back. She knows all about it.'

John could find nothing to say.

'It's not the first time,' Dr. Mackenzie continued. 'that I've been consulted by patients who have told me their symptoms and said they had come on behalf of friends or relations. It's an interesting feature of your case that you should want to ascribe the trouble to someone else, probably the decisive feature. I've given your wife the name of a man in London who I think will be able to help you. Meanwhile I can advise plenty of exercise, light meals at night. . . .'

John Verney limped back to Good Hope Fort in a state of consternation. Security had been compromised; the operation must be cancelled; initiative had been lost . . . all the phrases of the tactical school came to his mind, but he was still numb after this unexpected reverse. A vast and naked horror peeped at him and was thrust aside.

When he got back Elizabeth was laying the supper table. He stood on the balcony and stared at the gaping rails with eyes smarting with disappointment. It was dead calm that evening. The rising tide lapped and fell and mounted again silently among the rocks below. He stood gazing down, then he turned back into the room.

There was one large drink left in the whisky bottle. He poured it out and swallowed it. Elizabeth brought in the supper and they sat down. Gradually his mind grew a little calmer. They usually ate in silence. At last he said: 'Elizabeth, why did you tell the doctor I had been walking in my sleep?'

She quietly put down the plate she had been holding and looked at him curiously. 'Why?' she said gently. 'Because I was worried, of course. I didn't think you knew about it.'

'But have I been?'

'Oh yes, several times—in London and here. I didn't think it mattered at first, but the night before last I found you on the balcony, quite near that dreadful hole in the rails. I was really frightened. But it's going to be all right now. Dr. Mackenzie has given me the name. . . .'

It was possible, thought John Verney; nothing was more likely.

He had lived night and day for ten days thinking of that opening, of the sea and rock below, the ragged ironwork and the sharp edge of stone. He suddenly felt defeated, sick and stupid, as he had as he lay on the Italian hillside with his smashed knee. Then as now he had felt weariness even more than pain.

'Coffee, darling.'

Suddenly he roused himself. 'No,' he almost shouted. 'No, no, no.'

'Darling, what is the matter? Don't get excited. Are you feeling ill? Lie down on the sofa near the window.'

He did as he was told. He felt so weary that he could barely move from his chair.

'Do you think coffee would keep you awake, love? You look quite fit to drop already. There, lie down.'

He lay down, like the tide slowly mounting among the rocks below, sleep rose and spread in his mind. He nodded and woke with a start.

'Shall I open the window, darling, and give you some air?'

'Elizabeth,' he said, 'I feel as if I have been drugged.' Like the rocks below the window—now awash, now emerging clear from falling water; now awash again deeper; now barely visible, mere patches on the face of gentle eddying foam—his brain was softly drowning. He roused himself, as children do in nightmare, still scared, still half asleep. 'I can't be drugged,' he said loudly, 'I never touched the coffee.'

'Drugs in the coffee?' said Elizabeth gently, like a nurse soothing a fractious child, 'Drugs in the coffee? What an absurd idea. That's the kind of thing that only happens on the films, darling.'

He did not hear her. He was fast asleep, snoring stertorously by the open window.

Phyllis Bottome

PHYLLIS BOTTOME, who died in 1963 at the age of eighty-one, had her first novel published when she was only seventeen. By then she had already travelled widely in both Europe and America. She travelled all her life, spending thirty-nine years abroad, and living in seven different countries.

She became intensely interested in psychology and began to study under Dr. Alfred Adler. As a result she wrote *Private Worlds* which was made into a famous all-star film, while its title has become an accepted part of the language of psychology.

In her early years Miss Bottome was a best-selling author in the U.S.A., although in this country she was almost unknown. She continued to write throughout her life, nine of her books being published when she was over seventy.

HENRY

FOR FOUR hours every morning, and for twenty minutes before a large audience at night, Fletcher was locked up with murder.

It glared at him from twelve pairs of amber eyes; it clawed the air close to him, it spat naked hate at him, and watched with uninterrupted intensity, to catch him for one moment off his guard.

Fletcher had only his will and eyes to keep death at bay.

Of course, outside the cage, into which Fletcher shut himself nightly with his twelve tigers, were the keepers, standing at intervals around it with concealed pistols; but they were outside it. The idea was that if anything happened to Fletcher they would be able by prompt action to get him out alive; but they had his private instructions to do nothing of the kind, to

shoot straight at his heart, and pick off the guilty tiger afterwards to cover their intentions. Fletcher knew better than to
try to preserve anything the tigers left of him, if once they
started to attack.

The lion-tamer in the next cage was better off than Fletcher;
he was intoxicated by a rowdy vanity which dimmed fear.
He stripped himself half-naked every night, covered himself
with ribbons, and thought so much of himself that he hardly
noticed his lions. Besides, his lions had all been born in captivity,
were slightly doped; and were only lions.

Fletcher's tigers weren't doped because dope dulled their
fear of the whip and didn't dull their ferocity; captivity softened
nothing in them, and they hated man.

Fletcher had taught tigers since he was a child, his father had
started him on baby tigers, who were charming. They hurt
you as much as they could with an absent-minded roguishness
difficult to resist; what was death to you was play to them; but
as they couldn't kill him, all the baby tigers did was to harden
Fletcher and teach him to move about quickly. Speed is the
tiger's long suit, and Fletcher learned to beat them at it. He
knew by a long-trained instinct when a tiger was going to
move, and moved quicker so as to be somewhere else. He
learned that tigers must be treated like an audience, though for
different reasons; you must not turn your back upon them,
because tigers associate backs with springs.

Fletcher's swift eyes moved with the flickering sureness of
lightning—even quicker than lightning, for while lightning
has the leisure to strike, Fletcher had to avoid being struck by
something as quick as a flash and much more terrible.

For a few months the baby tigers could only be taught by
fear, fear of a whiplash, fear of a pocket pistol which stung
them with blank cartridges; and above all the mysterious fear
of the human eye. Fletcher's father used to make him sit

opposite him for hours practising eyes. When he was only ten years old, Fletcher had learned never to show a tiger that he was afraid of him. 'If you ain't afraid of a tiger, you're a fool,' his father told him; 'but if you show a tiger you're afraid of him, you won't even be a fool long!'

The first thing Fletcher taught his tigers, one by one in their cages, was to catch his eye, then he stared them down. He had to show them that his power of mesmerism was stronger than theirs; if once they believed this, they might believe that his power to strike was also stronger. Once Fletcher had accustomed tigers to be out-faced, he could stay in their cages for hours in comparative safety.

The next stage was to get them used to noise and light. Tigers dislike noise and light, and they wanted to take it out of Fletcher when he exposed them to it.

When it came to the actual trick teaching, Fletcher relied on his voice and long stinging whip. The lion-tamer roared at his lions; Fletcher's voice was not loud; but it was as noticeable as a warning bell, it checked his tigers like the crack of a pistol.

For four hours every morning, Fletcher, who was as kind as he was intrepid, frightened his tigers into doing tricks. He rewarded them as well; after they had been frightened enough to sit on tubs, he threw bits of raw meat. He wanted them to associate tubs with pieces of raw meat, and not sitting on tubs with whips; attempting to attack him, which they did during all transition stages, he wanted them to associate with flashes from his pocket pistol, followed by the impact of very unpleasant sensations. Their dislike of the pistol was an important point; they had to learn to dislike it so much that they would, for the sake of their dislike, sacrifice their fond desire to obliterate Fletcher.

Fletcher took them out one by one at first and then rehearsed them gradually together. It was during the single lessons that he discovered Henry.

Henry had been bought, rather older than the other tigers, from a drunken sailor. The drunken sailor had tearfully persisted that Henry was not as other tigers, and that selling him at all was like being asked to part with a talented and only child.

"E 'as a 'eart!' Henry's first proprietor repeated over and over again.

Fletcher, however, suspected this fanciful statement of being a mere ruse to raise Henry's price, and watchfully disregarded its implications.

For some time afterwards, Henry bore out Fletcher's suspicions. He snarled at all the keepers, showed his teeth and clawed the air close to Fletcher's head exactly like the eleven other tigers, only with more vim. He was a very fine young tiger, exceptionally powerful and large; the polished corners of the Temple did not shine more brilliantly than the lustrous striped skin on Henry's back, and when his painted impassive face, heavy and expressionless as a Hindoo idol's, broke up into activity, the very devils believed and trembled. Fletcher believed, but he didn't tremble—he only sat longer and longer, closer and closer to Henry's cage, watching.

The first day he went inside, there seemed no good reason, either to Henry or to himself, why he should live to get out. The second day something curious happened. While he was attempting to outstare Henry, and Henry was stalking him to get between him and the cage door, a flash of something like recognition came into Henry's eyes, a kind of 'Hail fellow well met!' He stopped stalking and sat down. Fletcher held him firmly with his eyes; the great painted head sank down and the amber eyes blurred and closed under Fletcher's penetrating gaze. A loud noise filled the cage, a contented, pleasant noise.

4

Henry was purring! Fletcher's voice changed from the sharp, brief order like the crack of a whip into a persuasive, companionable drawl. Henry's eyes re-opened; he rose, stood rigid for a moment, and then slowly the rigidity melted out of his powerful form. Once more that answering look came into the tiger's eyes. He stared straight at Fletcher without blinking and jumped on his tub. He sat on it impassively, his tail waving, his great jaws closed. He eyed Fletcher attentively and without hate. Then Fletcher knew that this tiger was not as other tigers; not as any other tiger.

He threw down his whip, Henry never moved; he approached Henry, Henry lifted up his lip to snarl, thought better of it, and permitted the approach. Fletcher took his life in his hand and touched Henry. Henry snarled mildly, but his great claws remained closed; his eyes expressed nothing but a gentle warning, they simply said: 'You know I don't like being touched, be careful, I might have to claw you!' Fletcher gave a brief nod; he knew the margin of safety was slight, but he had a margin. He could do something with Henry.

Hour after hour every day he taught Henry, but he taught him without a pistol or a whip. It was unnecessary to use anything beyond his voice and his eyes. Henry read his eyes eagerly. When he failed to catch Fletcher's meaning, Fletcher's voice helped him out. Henry did not always understand even Fletcher's voice, but where he differed from other tigers was that he wished to understand; nor had he after the first recognition the slightest inclination to kill Fletcher.

He used to sit for hours at the back of his cage waiting for Fletcher. When he heard far off—unbelievably far off—the sound of Fletcher's step, he moved forward to the front of the cage and prowled restlessly to and fro till Fletcher unlocked the door and entered. Then Henry would crouch back a little, politely, from no desire to avoid his friend, but as a tribute to the superior power he felt in Fletcher. Directly Fletcher spoke, he came forward proudly and exchanged their wordless eye language.

Henry liked doing his tricks alone with Fletcher. He jumped on and off his tub following the mere wave of Fletcher's hand. He soon went further, jumped on a high stool and leapt through a large white paper disc held up by Fletcher. Although the disc looked as if he couldn't possibly get through it, yet the clean white sheet always yielded to his impact; he did get through it, blinking a little, but feeling a curious pride that he had faced the odious thing; and pleased Fletcher.

He let Fletcher sit on his back, though the mere touch of an alien creature was repulsive to him. But he stood perfectly still, his hair rising a little, his teeth bared, a growl half suffocated in his throat. He told himself it was Fletcher. He must control his impulse to fling him off and tear him up.

In all the rehearsals and performances in the huge arena full of strange noises, blocked with alien human beings, Henry led the other tigers; and although Fletcher's influence over him was weakened, he still recognized it. Fletcher seemed farther away from him at these times, less sympathetic and godlike, but Henry tried hard to follow the intense persuasive eyes and the brief emphatic voice; he would not lose touch even with this attenuated ghost of Fletcher.

It was with Henry and Henry alone that Fletcher dared his nightly stunt, dropped the whip and stick at his feet and let Henry do his tricks as he did them in his cage alone, with nothing beyond Fletcher's eyes and voice to control him. The other eleven tigers, beaten glaring and snarling on to their tubs, sat impassively despising Henry's unnatural docility. He had the chance they had always wanted, and he didn't take it—what kind of tiger was he?

But Henry ignored the other tigers. Reluctantly, standing

with all four feet together on his tub, he contemplated a further triumph. Fletcher stood before him, holding a stick between his hands and above his head; intimately, compellingly, through the language of his eyes Fletcher told Henry to jump from his tub over his head. What Fletcher said was: 'Come on, old thing! Jump! Come on! I'll duck in time. You won't hurt me! It's my stunt! Stretch your old paws together and jump!' And Henry jumped. He hated the dazzling lights, loathed the hard, unexpected, senseless sounds which followed his leap, and he was secretly terrified that he would land on Fletcher. But it was very satisfactory when after his rush through the air he found he hadn't touched Fletcher, but had landed on another tub carefully prepared for him; and Fletcher said to him as plainly as possible before he did the drawer trick with the other tigers: 'Well! You are a one-er and no mistake!'

The drawer trick was the worst of Fletcher's stunts. He had to put a table in the middle of the cage, and whip each tiger up to it. When he had them placed each on his tub around the table, he had to feed them with a piece of raw meat deftly thrown at the exact angle to reach the special tiger for which it was intended, and to avoid contact with eleven other tigers ripe to dispute this intention. Fletcher couldn't afford the slightest mistake or a fraction of delay. Each tiger had to have in turn his piece of raw meat, the drawer shut after it—and opened—the next morsel thrown exactly into the grasp of the next tiger, and so on, until the twelve were fed.

Fletcher always placed Henry at his back. Henry snatched in turn his piece of raw meat, but he made no attempt, as the other tigers always did, to take anyone else's; and Fletcher felt the safer for knowing that Henry was at his back. He counted on Henry's power to protect him more than he counted on the four keepers standing outside the cage with their pistols. More than once, when one of the tigers turned restive, Fletcher had found Henry, rigid, but very light on his toes, close to his side, between him and danger.

The circus manager spoke to Fletcher warningly about his foolish infatuation for Henry.

'Mark my words, Fletcher,' he said, 'the tiger doesn't live that wouldn't do you in if it could. You give Henry too many chances—one day he'll take one of them!'

But Fletcher only laughed. He knew Henry; he had seen the soul of the great tiger leap to his eyes and shine there in answer to his own eyes. A man does not kill his god, at least not willingly. Two thousand years ago he did some such thing, through ignorance; but Fletcher forgot this incident. Besides, on the whole he believed more in Henry than he did in his fellow men. This was not surprising, because Fletcher had very little time for human fellowship. When he was not teaching tigers not to kill him, he rested from the exhaustion of the nerves which comes from a prolonged companionship with eager, potential murderers. The rest of the time Fletcher boasted of Henry to the lion-tamer; and taught Henry new tricks.

Macormack, the lion-tamer, had a very good stunt lion, and he was extravagantly jealous of Henry. He could not make his lion go out backwards before him from the arena cage into the passage as Henry had learned to do before Fletcher; and when he had tried, Ajax had, not seriously but with an intention rather more than playful, flung him against the bars of the cage.

Macormack brooded deeply on this slight from his pet, and determined to take it out of Fletcher's.

'Pooh!' he said. 'You call yourself damned plucky for laying your ole 'oof on 'Enry's scruff, and 'e don't 'alf look wicked while you're doing it. Why don't yer put yer 'ead in 'is mouf and be done with it? That ud be talking, that would!'

'I wouldn't mind doing it,' said Fletcher reflectively, after a brief pause, 'once I get him used to the idea. 'Is jaw ain't so big as a lion's, still I could get the top of me 'ead in.'

The lion-tamer swaggered off jeering, and Fletcher thought out how best to lay this new trick before Henry for his approval.

But from the first Henry didn't approve of it. He showed quite plainly that he didn't want his head touched. He didn't like his mouth held forcibly open, and wouldn't have anything put between his teeth without crunching. Fletcher wasted several loaves of bread over the effort—and only succeeded once or twice gingerly and very ungracefully in getting portions of his own head in and out in safety. Henry roared long and loudly at him, clawed the air, and flashed all the language he could from his flaming eyes into Fletcher's, to explain that this thing wasn't done between tigers! It was hitting below the belt! An infringement of an instinct too deep for him to master; and Fletcher knew that he was outraging Henry's instinct, and decided to refrain.

'It ain't fair to my tiger!' he said to himself regretfully, and he soothed Henry with raw meat and endearments, promising to refrain from this unnatural venture.

But when the hour for performance came, Fletcher forgot his promise. He was enraged at Macormack's stunt lion for getting more than his share of the applause. He had the middle cage, and what with the way Macormack swaggered half-naked in his scarlet ribbons, and the lion roared—that pulverizing, deep-toned, desert roar—and yet did all his tricks one after the other like a little gentleman, it did seem as if Henry barely got a round of his due applause.

Henry jumped through his white disc—so did the stunt lion. He took his leap over Fletcher's head—the stunt lion did something flashy with a drum, not half as dangerous, and the blind and ignorant populace ignored Henry and preferred the drum.

'I don't care!' said Fletcher to himself. 'Henry's got to take my head in his mouth whether he likes it or not—that'll startle 'em!'

He got rid of all the other tigers. Henry was used to that, he liked it; now he would do his own final stunt—walk out backwards into the passage which led to the cages, and Fletcher would hurry out through the arena and back to Henry's cage, give him a light extra supper, and tell him what a fine tiger he was.

But Fletcher called him into the middle of the stage instead and made him take that terrible attitude he had taught him for the new trick. His eyes said: 'You'll do this once for me, old man, won't you?'

Henry's eyes said: 'Don't ask it! I'm tired! I'm hungry! I want to get out!'

But Fletcher couldn't read Henry's eyes any more. He tried to force his head sideways into the terrible open jaws, and Henry's teeth, instinctive, reluctant, compelled, closed on Fletcher's neck.

What Henry minded after the momentary relief of his instinctive action was the awful stillness of Fletcher. It wasn't the stillness of the arena—that was nothing, a mere deep indrawn breath. Fletcher lay limp between his paws, as if the trick were over, as if all tricks were over. He wouldn't get up, he didn't look at Henry. Henry's eyes gazed down unblinkingly into the blank eyes of Fletcher. All Henry's soul was in his eyes watching for Fletcher's soul to rise to meet them. And for an age nothing happened until at last Henry realized that nothing ever would.

Before the nearest keeper shot Henry, Henry knew that he had killed his god. He lifted up his heavy painted head and roared out through the still arena, a loud despairing cry.

His heart was pierced before the bullet reached it.

Dorothy L. Sayers

DOROTHY L. SAYERS died in 1958, at the age of sixty-five. She was the daughter of the Rev. Henry Sayers, who was, at one time, Head-master of the Cathedral Choir School in Oxford. Her mother was a niece of Percival Leigh, 'The Professor' of Punch, who acted with Dickens and was a friend of Thackeray.

After a time as a first-line copy writer with a London advertising agency, Dorothy Sayers took up writing as a career. She became famous for her crime stories, and for her creation of Lord Peter Wimsey, the amateur detective who featured in many of her books.

Later she became equally well known as a writer of religious plays.

THE MAN WHO KNEW HOW

FOR PERHAPS the twentieth time since the train had left Carlisle, Pender glanced up from *Murder at the Manse* and caught the eye of the man opposite.

He frowned a little. It was irritating to be watched so closely, and always with the faint, sardonic smile. It was still more irritating to allow oneself to be so much disturbed by the smile and the scrutiny. Pender wrenched himself back to his book with a determination to concentrate upon the problem of the minister murdered in the library.

But the story was of the academic kind that crowds all its exciting incidents into the first chapter, and proceeds thereafter by a long series of deductions to a scientific solution in the last. The thin thread of interest, spun precariously upon the wheel of Pender's reasoning brain, had been snapped. Twice he had to turn back to verify points that he had missed in reading.

Then he became aware that his eyes had followed three closely argued pages without conveying anything whatever to his intelligence.

He was not thinking about the murdered minister at all—he was becoming more and more actively conscious of the other man's face.

A queer face, Pender thought.

There was nothing especially remarkable about the features in themselves; it was their expression that daunted Pender. It was a secret face, the face of one who knew a great deal to other people's disadvantage. The mouth was a little crooked and tightly tucked in at the corners as though savouring a hidden amusement. The eyes, behind a pair of rimless pince-nez, glittered curiously; but that was possibly due to the light reflected in the glasses.

Pender wondered what the man's profession might be. He was dressed in a dark lounge suit, a raincoat, and a shabby soft hat; his age was perhaps about forty.

Pender coughed unnecessarily and settled back into his corner, raising the detective story high before his face, barrier fashion. This was worse than useless. He gained the impression that the man saw through the manoeuvre and was secretly entertained by it. He wanted to fidget, but felt obscurely that his doing so would in some way constitute a victory for the other man.

In his self-consciousness he held himself so rigid that attention to his book became a sheer physical impossibility.

There was no stop now before Rugby, and it was unlikely that any passenger would enter from the corridor to break up this disagreeable *solitude à deux*. But something must be done. The silence had lasted so long that any remark, however trivial, would—so Pender felt—burst upon the tense atmosphere with the unnatural clatter of an alarm clock. One could, of course, go out into the corridor and not return, but that would be acknowledging defeat.

Pender lowered *Murder at the Manse* and caught the man's eye again.

'Getting tired of it?' asked the man.

'Night journeys are always a bit tedious,' replied Pender, half relieved and half reluctant. 'Would you like a book?'

He took *The Paper-clip Clue* from his attache case and held it out hopefully. The other man glanced at the title and shook his head.

'Thanks very much,' he said, 'but I never read detective stories. They're so inadequate, don't you think so?'

'They are rather lacking in characterization and human interest, certainly,' said Pender, 'but on a railway journey——'

'I don't mean that,' said the other man. 'I am not concerned with humanity. But all those murderers are so incompetent—they bore me.'

'Oh, I don't know,' replied Pender. 'At any rate they are usually a good deal more imaginative and ingenious than murderers in real life.'

'Than the murderers who are found out in real life, yes,' admitted the other man.

'Even some of those did pretty well before they got pinched,' objected Pender. 'Crippen, for instance; he need never have been caught if he hadn't lost his head and run off to America. George Joseph Smith did away with at least two brides quite successfully before fate and the *News of the World* intervened.'

'Yes,' said the other man, 'but look at the clumsiness of it all; the elaboration, the lies, the paraphernalia. Absolutely unnecessary.'

'Oh, come!' said Pender. 'You can't expect committing a murder and getting away with it to be as simple as shelling peas.'

'Ah!' said the other man. 'You think that, do you?'

Pender waited for him to elaborate his remark, but nothing came of it. The man leaned back and smiled in his secret way at the roof of the carriage; he appeared to think the conversation not worth going on with. Pender, taking up his book again, found himself attracted by his companion's hands. They were white and surprisingly long in the fingers. He watched them gently tapping upon their owner's knee—then resolutely turned a page—then put the book down once more and said:

'Well, if it's so easy, how would *you* set about committing a murder?'

'I?' repeated the man. The light on his glasses made his eyes quite blank to Pender, but his voice sounded gently amused. 'That's different; I should not have to think twice about it.'

'Why not?'

'Because I happen to know how to do it.'

'Do you indeed?' muttered Pender, rebelliously.

'Oh, yes; there's nothing in it.'

'How can you be sure? You haven't tried, I suppose?'

'It isn't a case of trying,' said the man. 'There's nothing tentative about my method. That's just the beauty of it.'

'It's easy to say that,' retorted Pender, 'but what *is* this wonderful method?'

'You can't expect me to tell you that, can you?' said the other man, bringing his eyes back to rest on Pender's face. 'It might not be safe. You look harmless enough, but who could look more harmless than Crippen? Nobody is fit to be trusted with *absolute* control over other people's lives.'

'Bosh!' exclaimed Pender. 'I shouldn't think of murdering anybody.'

'Oh, yes, you would,' said the other man, 'if you really believed it was safe. So would anybody. Why are all these tremendous artificial barriers built up round murder by the

Church and the law? Just because it's everybody's crime, and just as natural as breathing.'

'But that's ridiculous!' cried Pender, warmly.

'You think so, do you? That's what most people would say. But I wouldn't trust 'em. Not with sulphate of thanatol to be bought for twopence at any chemist's.'

'Sulphate of what?' asked Pender, sharply.

'Ah! You think I'm giving something away. Well, it's a mixture of that and one or two other things—all equally ordinary and cheap. For ninepence you could make up enough to poison the entire House of Commons—and even you would hardly call that a crime, would you? But of course one wouldn't polish the whole lot off at once; it might look funny if they all died simultaneously in their baths.'

'Why in their baths?'

'That's the way it would take them. It's the action of the hot water that brings on the effect of the stuff, you see. Any time from a few hours to a few days after administration. It's quite a simple chemical reaction and it couldn't possibly be detected by analysis. It would just look like heart failure.'

Pender eyed him uneasily. He did not like the smile; it was not only derisive, it was smug, it was almost—gloating—triumphant! He could not quite put a name to it.

'You know,' pursued the man, thoughtfully pulling a pipe from his pocket and beginning to fill it, 'it is very odd how often one seems to read of people being found dead in their baths. It must be a very common accident. Quite temptingly so. After all, there is a fascination about murder. The thing grows upon one—that is, I imagine it would, you know.'

'Very likely,' said Pender.

'Look at Palmer. Look at Gesina Gottfried. Look at Armstrong. No, I wouldn't trust anybody with that formula—not even a virtuous young man like yourself.'

The long white fingers tamped the tobacco firmly into the bowl and struck a match.

'But how about you?' said Pender, irritated. (Nobody cares to be called a virtuous young man.) 'If nobody is fit to be trusted——'

'I'm not, eh?' replied the man. 'Well, that's true, but it's past praying for now, isn't it? I know the thing and I can't unknow it again. It's unfortunate, but there it is. At any rate you have the comfort of knowing that nothing disagreeable is likely to happen to *me*. Dear me! Rugby already. I get out here. I have a little business to do at Rugby.'

He rose and shook himself, buttoned his raincoat about him, and pulled the shabby hat more firmly down above his enigmatic glasses. The train slowed down and stopped. With a brief good-night and a crooked smile the man stepped on to the platform. Pender watched him stride quickly away into the drizzle beyond the radius of the gas-light.

'Dotty or something,' said Pender, oddly relieved. 'Thank goodness, I seem to be going to have the carriage to myself.'

He returned to *Murder at the Manse*, but his attention still kept wandering.

'What was the name of that stuff the fellow talked about?' For the life of him he could not remember.

It was on the following afternoon that Pender saw the news item. He had bought the *Standard* to read at lunch, and the word 'bath' caught his eye; otherwise he would probably have missed the paragraph altogether, for it was only a short one.

WEALTHY MANUFACTURER DIES IN BATH
WIFE'S TRAGIC DISCOVERY

A distressing discovery was made early this morning by Mrs. John Brittlesea, wife of the well-known head of Brittlesea's Engineering works at Rugby. Finding that her husband, whom she had seen alive and well less than an hour previously, did not come down in time for breakfast, she searched for him in the bathroom, where, on the

door being broken down, the engineer was found lying dead in his
bath, life having been extinct, according to medical men, for half
an hour. The cause of the death is pronounced to be heart failure.
The deceased manufacturer. . . .

'That's an odd coincidence,' said Pender. 'At Rugby. I
should think my unknown friend would be interested—if he is
still there doing his bit of business. I wonder what his business
is, by the way.'

It is a very curious thing how, when once your attention is
attracted to any particular set of circumstances, that set of circumstances seems to haunt you. You get appendicitis: immediately the newspapers are filled with paragraphs about statesmen
suffering from appendicitis and victims dying of it; you learn
that all your acquaintances have had it, or know friends who
have had it, and either died of it, or recovered from it with
more surprising and spectacular rapidity than yourself; you
cannot open a popular magazine without seeing its cure mentioned as one of the triumphs of modern surgery, or dip into a
scientific treatise without coming across a comparison of the
vermiform appendix in men and monkeys.

Probably these references to appendicitis are equally frequent
at all times, but you only notice them when your mind is
attuned to the subject. At any rate, it was in this way that
Pender accounted to himself for the extraordinary frequency
with which people seemed to die in their baths at this period.

The thing pursued him at every turn. Always the same
sequence of events: the hot bath, the discovery of the corpse,
the inquest; always the same medical opinion; heart failure
following immersion in too-hot water. It began to seem to
Pender that it was scarcely safe to enter a hot bath at all. He
took to making his own bath cooler every day, until it almost
ceased to be enjoyable.

He skimmed his paper each morning for headlines about

baths before settling down to read the news; and was at once relieved and vaguely disappointed if a week passed without a hot-bath tragedy.

One of the sudden deaths that occurred in this way was that of a young and beautiful woman whose husband, an analytical chemist, had tried without success to divorce her a few months previously. The coroner displayed a tendency to suspect foul play and put the husband through a severe cross-examination. There seemed, however, to be no getting behind the doctor's evidence.

Pender, brooding fancifully over the improbable possible, wished, as he did every day of the week, that he could remember the name of that drug the man in the train had mentioned.

Then came the excitement in Pender's own neighbourhood. An old Mr. Skimmings, who lived alone with a housekeeper in a street just round the corner, was found dead in his bathroom. His heart had never been strong. The housekeeper told the milkman that she had always expected something of the sort to happen, for the old gentleman would always take his bath so hot.

Pender went to the inquest.

The housekeeper gave her evidence. Mr. Skimmings had been the kindest of employers, and she was heartbroken at losing him. No, she had not been aware that Mr. Skimmings had left her a large sum of money, but it was just like his goodness of heart. The verdict was Death by Misadventure.

Pender, that evening, went out for his usual stroll with the dog. Some feelings of curiosity moved him to go round past the late Mr. Skimmings' house. As he loitered by, glancing up at the blank windows, the garden gate opened and a man came out. In the light of a street lamp, Pender recognized him at once.

'Hullo!' he said.

'Oh, it's you, is it?' said the man. 'Viewing the site of the tragedy, eh? What do you think about it all?'

'Oh, nothing very much,' said Pender. 'I didn't know him. Odd, our meeting again like this.'

'Yes, isn't it? You live near here, I suppose.'

'Yes,' said Pender; and then wished he hadn't. 'Do you live in these parts too?'

'Me?' said the man. 'Oh, no. I was only here on a little matter of business.'

'Last time we met,' said Pender, 'you had business at Rugby.' They had fallen in step together, and were walking slowly down to the turning Pender had to take in order to reach his house.

'So I had,' agreed the man. 'My business takes me all over the country. I never know where I may be wanted next.'

'It was while you were at Rugby that old Brittlesea was found dead in his bath, wasn't it?' remarked Pender, carelessly.

'Yes. Funny thing, coincidence.' The man glanced up at him sideways through his glittering glasses. 'Left all his money to his wife, didn't he? She's a rich woman now. Good-looking girl—a lot younger than he was.'

They were passing Pender's gate. 'Come in and have a drink,' said Pender, and again immediately regretted the impulse.

The man accepted, and they went into Pender's bachelor study.

'Remarkable lot of these bath-deaths there have been lately, haven't there?' observed Pender carelessly, as he splashed soda into the tumblers.

'You think it's remarkable?' said the man, with his usual irritating trick of querying everything that was said to him. 'Well, I don't know. Perhaps it is. But it's a fairly common accident.'

'I suppose I've been taking more notice on account of that

conversation we had in the train.' Pender laughed, a little self-consciously. 'It just makes me wonder—you know how one does—whether anybody else had happened to hit on that drug you mentioned—what was its name?'

The man ignored the question.

'Oh, I shouldn't think so,' he said. 'I fancy I'm the only person who knows about that. I only stumbled on the thing by accident myself when I was looking for something else. I don't imagine it could have been discovered simultaneously in so many parts of the country. But all these verdicts just show, don't they, what a safe way it would be of getting rid of a person.'

'You're a chemist, then?' asked Pender, catching at the one phrase which seemed to promise information.

'Oh, I'm a bit of everything. Sort of general utility man. I do a good bit of studying on my own, too. You've got one or two interesting books here, I see.'

Pender was flattered. For a man in his position—he had been in a bank until he came into that little bit of money—he felt that he had improved his mind to some purpose, and he knew that his collection of modern first editions would be worth money some day. He went over to the glass-fronted book-case and pulled out a volume or two to show his visitor.

The man displayed intelligence, and presently joined him in front of the shelves. 'These, I take it, represent your personal tastes?' He took down a volume of Henry James and glanced at the fly-leaf. 'That your name? E. Pender?'

Pender admitted that it was. 'You have the advantage of me,' he added.

'Oh! I am one of the great Smith clan,' said the other with a laugh, 'and work for my bread. You seem to be very nicely fixed here.'

Pender explained about the clerkship and the legacy.

'Very nice, isn't it?' said Smith. 'Not married? No. You're one of the lucky ones. Not likely to be needing any sulphate of . . . any useful drugs in the near future. And you never will, if you stick to what you've got and keep off women and speculation.'

He smiled up sideways at Pender. Now that his hat was off, Pender saw that he had a quantity of closely curled grey hair, which made him look older than he had appeared in the railway carriage.

'No, I shan't be coming to you for assistance yet awhile,' said Pender, laughing. 'Besides, how should I find you if I wanted you?'

'You wouldn't have to,' said Smith. 'I should find *you*. There's never any difficulty about that.' He grinned, oddly. 'Well I'd better be getting on. Thank you for your hospitality. I don't expect we shall meet again—but we may, of course. Things work out so queerly, don't they?'

When he had gone, Pender returned to his own armchair. He took up his glass of whisky, which stood there nearly full.

'Funny!' he said to himself. 'I don't remember pouring that out. I suppose I got interested and did it mechanically.' He emptied his glass slowly, thinking about Smith.

What in the world was Smith doing at Skimmings' house?

An odd business altogether. If Skimmings' housekeeper had known about that money. . . . But she had not known, and if she had, how could she have found out about Smith and his sulphate of . . . the word had been on the tip of his tongue then.

'You would not need to find me. I should find *you*.' What had the man meant by that? But this was ridiculous. Smith was not the devil, presumably. But if he really had this secret—if he liked to put a price upon it—nonsense!'

'Business at Rugby—a little bit of business at Skimmings' house.' Oh, absurd!

'Nobody is fit to be trusted. *Absolute* power over another man's life . . . it grows on you.'

Lunacy! And, if there was anything in it, the man was mad to tell Pender about it. If Pender chose to speak he could get the fellow hanged. The very existence of Pender would be dangerous.

That whisky!

More and more, thinking it over, Pender became persuaded that he had never poured it out. Smith must have done it while his back was turned. Why that sudden display of interest in the bookshelves? It had no connection with anything that had gone before. Now Pender came to think of it, it had been a very stiff whisky. Was it imagination, or had there been something about the flavour of it? A cold sweat broke out on Pender's forehead.

A quarter of an hour later, after a powerful dose of mustard and water, Pender was downstairs again, very cold and shivering, huddling over the fire. He had had a narrow escape—if he had escaped. He did not know how the stuff worked, but he would not take a hot bath again for some days. One never knew.

Whether the mustard and water had done the trick in time, or whether the hot bath was an essential part of the treatment, at any rate Pender's life was saved for the time being. But he was still uneasy. He kept the front door on the chain and warned his servant to let no strangers into the house.

He ordered two more morning papers and the *News of the World* on Sundays, and kept a careful watch upon their columns. Deaths in baths became an obsession with him. He neglected his first editions and took to attending inquests.

Three weeks later he found himself at Lincoln. A man had died of heart failure in a Turkish bath—a fat man of sedentary habits. The jury added a rider to their verdict of Misadventure to the effect that the management should exercise a stricter supervision over the bathers and should never permit them to be left unattended in the hot room.

As Pender emerged from the hall he saw ahead of him a shabby hat that seemed familiar. He plunged after it, and caught Mr. Smith about to step into a taxi.

'Smith,' he cried, gasping a little. He clutched him fiercely by the shoulder.

'What, you again?' said Smith. 'Taking notes of the case, eh? *Can I do anything for you?*'

'You devil!' said Pender. 'You're mixed up in this! You tried to kill me the other day.'

'Did I? Why should I do that?'

'You'll swing for this,' shouted Pender, menacingly.

A policeman pushed his way through the gathering crowd. 'Here,' said he, 'What's all this about?'

Smith touched his forehead significantly.

'It's all right, officer,' said he. 'The gentleman seems to think I'm here for no good. Here's my card. The coroner knows me. You'd better keep an eye on him.'

'That's right,' said a bystander.

'This man tried to kill me,' said Pender.

The policeman nodded. 'Don't you worry about that, sir,' he said. 'You think better of it. The 'eat in there has upset you a bit. All right, *all* right.'

'But I want to charge him,' said Pender.

'I wouldn't do that if I was you,' said the policeman.

'I tell you,' said Pender, that this man Smith has been trying to poison me. He's poisoned scores of people.'

The policeman winked at Smith. 'Best be off, sir,' he said. 'I'll settle this. Now, my lad'—and he held Pender firmly by the arms—just you keep cool and take it quiet. The gentleman's name ain't Smith nor nothing like it. You've got a bit mixed up like.'

'Well, what is his name?' demanded Pender.

'Never you mind,' replied the constable. 'You leave him alone, or you'll be getting yourself into trouble.'

The taxi had driven away. Pender glanced round at the circle of amused faces and gave in.

'All right, officer,' he said. 'I won't give you any trouble. I'll come round to the police station and tell you about it.'

'What do you think o' that one?' asked the inspector of the sergeant when Pender had stumbled out of the station.

'Up the pole 'an 'alfway round the flag, if you ask me,' replied his subordinate. 'Got one of them ideez fix what they talk about.'

'H'm!' replied the inspector. 'Well, we've got his name and address. Better make a note of 'em. He might turn up again. Poisoning people so as they die in their baths, eh? That's a good 'un. Wonderful how these barmy ones think it all out, isn't it?'

The spring that year was a bad one—cold and foggy. It was March when Pender went down to an inquest at Deptford, but a thick blanket of mist was hanging over the river as though it were November. The cold ate into your bones. As he sat in the dingy little court, peering through the yellow twilight of gas and fog, he could scarcely see the witnesses as they came to the table. Everybody in the place seemed to be coughing too. His bones ached, and he felt as though he were about due for a bout of influenza.

Straining his eyes, he thought he recognized a face on the other side of the room, but the smarting fog which penetrated every crack stung and blinded him. He felt in his overcoat pocket, and his hand closed comfortably on something thick and heavy. Ever since that day in Lincoln he had gone about armed for protection. Not a revolver—he was no hand with firearms. A sandbag was much better. He had bought one from an old man wheeling a barrow. It was meant for keeping out draughts from the door—a good, old-fashioned affair.

The inevitable verdict was returned. The spectators began to push their way out. Pender had to hurry now, not to lose sight of his man. He elbowed his way along, muttering apologies. At the door he almost touched the man, but a stout woman intervened. He plunged past her, and she gave a little squeak of indignation. The man in front turned his head, and the light over the door glinted on his glasses.

Pender pulled his hat over his eyes and followed. His shoes had crepe rubber soles and made no sound on the sticky pavement. The man went on, jogging quietly up one street and down another, and never looking back. The fog was so thick that Pender was forced to keep within a few yards of him. Where was he going? Into the lighted streets? Home by bus or tram?

No. He turned off to the left, down a narrow street.

The fog was thicker there. Pender could no longer see his quarry, but he heard the footsteps going on before him at the same even pace. It seemed to him that they two were alone in the world—pursued and pursuer, slayer and avenger. The street began to slope more rapidly. They must be coming out near the river.

Suddenly the dim shapes of the houses fell away on either side. There was an open space with a lamp vaguely visible in the middle. The footsteps paused. Pender, silently hurrying after, saw the man standing close beneath the lamp, apparently consulting something in a notebook.

Four steps and Pender was upon him. He drew the sandbag from his pocket. The man looked up.

'I've got you this time,' said Pender, and struck with all his force.

Pender had been quite right. He did get influenza. It was a

week before he was out and about again. The weather had changed, and the air was fresh and sweet. In spite of the weakness left by the malady he felt as though a heavy weight had been lifted from his shoulders. He tottered down to a favourite bookshop of his in the Strand, and picked up a D. H. Lawrence 'first' at a price which he knew to be a bargain. Encouraged by this, he turned into a small chop-house, chiefly frequented by Fleet Street men, and ordered a grilled cutlet, and a half-tankard of bitter.

Two journalists were seated at the next table.

'Going to poor old. Buckley's funeral?' asked one.

'Yes,' said the other. 'Poor devil. Fancy his getting sloshed on the head like that. He must have been on his way down to interview the widow of that fellow who died in a bath. It's a rough district. Probably one of Jimmy the Card's crowd had it in for him. He was a great crime-reporter—they won't get another like Bill Buckley in a hurry.'

'He was a decent sort, too. Great old sport. No end of a leg-puller. Remember his great stunt about sulphate of thanatol?'

Pender started. *That* was the word that had eluded him for so many months. A curious dizziness came over him and he took a pull at the tankard to steady himself.

'. . . looking at you as sober as a judge,' the journalist was saying. 'He used to work off that wheeze on poor boobs in railway carriages to see how they'd take it. Would you believe that one chap actually offered him——'

'Hullo,' interrupted his friend. 'The bloke over there has fainted. I thought he was looking a bit white.'

Daphne du Maurier

DAPHNE DU MAURIER is married to Lt-Gen. Sir Frederick Browning, wartime commander of the Airborne Forces, and later Treasurer to the Duke of Edinburgh.

Together they live in the beautiful house of Menabilly, near Fowey in Cornwall. The house with its secret panels and hidden passages is reputed to have been the haunt of smugglers, and local gossip has it that during the Civil War prisoners were bricked up inside the hollow walls, and left to die.

Not surprisingly, three of her most popular novels were inspired by the romance of this old house.

After writing *Rebecca* and *Jamaica Inn*, Daphne du Maurier suddenly found herself, to her great surprise, one of the most popular authors of the day. There followed *Frenchman's Creek*, *My Cousin Rachel*, and *The King's General*.

Her work appears in more than twenty languages, and many of her stories have been filmed, starring such famous actors as Laurence Olivier, and such producers as Alfred Hitchcock.

THE OLD MAN

DID I hear you asking about the Old Man? I thought so. You're a newcomer to the district, here on holiday. We get plenty these days, during the summer months. Somehow they always find their way eventually over the cliffs down to this beach, and then they pause and look from the sea back to the lake. Just as you did.

It's a lovely spot, isn't it? Quiet and remote. You can't wonder at the old man choosing to live here.

I don't remember when he first came. Nobody can. Many

years ago, it must have been. He was here when I arrived, long before the war. Perhaps he came to escape from civilization, much as I did myself. Or maybe, where he lived before, the folks around made things too hot for him. It's hard to say. I had the feeling, from the very first, that he had done something, or something had been done to him, that gave him a grudge against the world. I remember the first time I set eyes on him I said to myself, 'I bet that old fellow is one hell of a character.'

Yes, he was living here beside the lake, along of his missus. Funny sort of lash-up they had, exposed to all weather, but they didn't seem to mind.

I had been warned about him by one of the fellows from the farm, who advised me, with a grin, to give the old man who lived down by the lake a wide berth—he didn't care for strangers. So I went warily, and I didn't stay to pass the time of day. Nor would it have been any use if I had, not knowing a word of his lingo. The first time I saw him he was standing by the edge of the lake, looking out to sea, and from tact I avoided the piece of planking over the stream, which meant passing close to him, and crossed to the other side of the lake by the beach instead. Then, with an awkward feeling that I was trespassing and had no business to be there, I bobbed down behind a clump of gorse, took out my spy-glass, and had a peep at him.

He was a big fellow, broad and strong—he's aged, of course, lately; I'm speaking of several years back—but even now you can see what he must have been once. Such power and drive behind him, and that fine head, which he carried like a king. There's an idea in that, too. No, I'm not joking. Who knows what royal blood he carries inside him, harking back to some remote ancestor? And now and again, surging in him—not through his own fault—it gets the better of him and drives him fighting mad. I didn't think about that at the time. I just looked at him, and ducked behind the gorse when I saw him turn, and I wondered to myself what went on in his mind, whether he knew I was there, watching him.

If he should decide to come up the lake after me I should look pretty foolish. He must have thought better of it, though, or perhaps he did not care. He went on staring out to sea, watching the gulls and the incoming tide, and presently he ambled off his side of the lake, heading for the missus and home and maybe supper.

I didn't catch a glimpse of her that first day. She just wasn't around. Living as they do, close in by the left bank of the lake, with no proper track to the place, I hardly had the nerve to venture close and come upon her face to face. When I did see her, though, I was disappointed. She wasn't much to look at after all. What I mean is, she hadn't got anything like his character. A placid, mild-tempered creature, I judged her.

They had both come back from fishing when I saw them, and were making their way up from the beach to the lake. He was in front, of course. She tagged along behind. Neither of them took the slightest notice of me, and I was glad, because the old man might have paused, and waited, and told her to get on back home, and then come down towards the rocks where I was sitting. You ask what I would have said, had he done so? I'm damned if I know. Maybe I would have got up, whistling and seemingly unconcerned, and then, with a nod and a smile—useless, really, but instinctive, if you know what I mean—said good day and pottered off. I don't think he would have done anything. He'd just have stared after me, with those strange narrow eyes of his, and let me go.

After that, winter and summer, I was always down on the beach or the rocks, and they went on living their curious, remote existence, sometimes fishing in the lake, sometimes at sea. Occasionally I'd come across them in the harbour on the estuary, taking a look at the yachts anchored there, and the shipping. I used to wonder which of them made the suggestion. Perhaps suddenly he would be lured by the thought of the bustle and life of the harbour, and all the things he had either wantonly given up or never known, and he would say to her, 'Today we are going into town.' And she, happy to do whatever pleased him best, followed along.

You see, one thing that stood out—and you couldn't help noticing it—was that the pair of them were devoted to one another. I've seen her greet him when he came back from a day's fishing and had left her back home, and towards evening she'd come down the lake and on to the beach and down to the sea to wait for him. She'd see him coming from a long way off, and I would see him too, rounding the corner of the bay. He'd come straight in to the beach, and she would go to meet him, and they would embrace each other, not caring a damn who saw them. It was touching, if you know what I mean. You felt there was something lovable about the old man, if that's how things were between them. He might be a devil to outsiders, but he was all the world to her. It gave me a warm feeling for him, when I saw them together like that.

You asked if they had any family? I was coming to that. It's about the family I really wanted to tell you. Because there was a tragedy, you see. And nobody knows anything about it except me. I suppose I could have told someone, but if I had, I don't know. . . . They might have taken the old man away, and she'd have broken her heart without him, and anyway, when all's said and done, it wasn't my business. I know the evidence against the old man was strong, but I hadn't positive proof it might have been some sort of accident, and anyway, nobody made any inquiries at the time the boy disappeared, so who was I to turn busybody and informer?

I'll try and explain what happened. But you must understand that all this took place over quite a time, and sometimes I was away from home or busy, and didn't go near the lake. Nobody seemed to take any interest in the couple living there but myself, so that it was only what I observed with my own eyes that makes this story, nothing that I heard from anybody else, no scraps of gossip, or tales told about them behind their backs.

Yes, they weren't always alone, as they are now. They had four kids. Three girls and a boy. They brought up the four of them in that ramshackle old place by the lake, and it was always a wonder to me how they did it. God, I've known days when the rain lashed the lake into little waves that burst and broke on the muddy shore near by their place, and turned the marsh into a swamp, and the wind driving straight in. You'd have thought anyone with a grain of sense would have taken his missus and his kids out of it and gone off somewhere where they could get some creature comforts at least. Not the old man. If he could stick it, I guess he decided she could too, and the kids as well. Maybe he wanted to bring them up the hard way.

Mark you, they were attractive youngsters. Especially the youngest girl, I never knew her name, but I called her Tiny, she had so much go to her. Chip off the old block, in spite of her size. I can see her now, as a little thing, the first to venture paddling in the lake, on a fine morning, way ahead of her sisters and the brother.

The brother I nicknamed Boy. He was the eldest, and between you and me a bit of a fool. He hadn't the looks of his sisters and was a clumsy sort of fellow. The girls would play around on their own, and go fishing, and he'd hang about in the background, not knowing what to do with himself. If he possibly could he'd stay around home, near his mother. Proper mother's boy. That's why I gave him the name. Not that she seemed to fuss over him any more than she did the others. She treated the four alike, as far as I could tell. Her thoughts were always for the old man rather than for them. But Boy was just a great baby, and I have an idea he was simple.

Like the parents, the youngsters kept themselves to themselves. Been dinned into them, I dare say, by the old man. They never came down to the beach on their own and played; and it must have been a temptation, I thought, in full summer, when people came walking over the cliffs down to the beach to bathe and picnic. I suppose, for those strange reasons best known to himself, the old man had warned them to have no truck with strangers.

They were used to me pottering, day in, day out, fetching driftwood and that. And often I would pause and watch the kids playing by the lake. I didn't talk to them, though. They might have gone back and told the old man. They used to look up when I passed by, then glance away again, sort of shy. All but Tiny. Tiny would toss her head and do a somersault, just to show off.

I sometimes watched them go off, the six of them—the old man, the missus, Boy, and the three girls, for a day's fishing out to sea. The old man, of course, in charge; Tiny eager to help, close to her dad; the missus looking about her to see if the weather was going to keep fine; the two other girls alongside; and Boy, poor simple Boy, always the last to leave home. I never knew what sport they had. They used to stay out late, and I'd have left the beach by the time they came back again. But I guess they did well. They must have lived almost entirely on what they caught. Well, fish is said to be full of vitamins, isn't it? Perhaps the old man was a food faddist in his way.

Time passed, and the youngsters began to grow up. Tiny lost something of her individuality then, it seemed to me. She grew more like her sisters. They were a nice-looking trio, all the same. Quiet, you know, well behaved.

As for Boy, he was enormous. Almost as big as the old man, but with what a difference! He had none of his father's looks, or strength, or personality; he was nothing but a great clumsy lout. And the trouble was, I believe the old man was ashamed of him. He didn't pull his weight in the home, I'm certain of that. And out fishing he was perfectly useless. The girls would work away like beetles, with Boy, always in the background, making a mess of things. If his mother was there he just stayed by her side.

I could see it rattled the old man to have such an oaf of a son. Irritated him, too, because Boy was so big. It probably didn't make sense to his intolerant mind. Strength and stupidity didn't go together. In any normal family, of course, Boy would have left home by now and gone out to work. I used to wonder if they argued about it back in the evenings, the missus and the old man, or if it was something never admitted between them but tacitly understood—Boy was no good.

Well, they did leave home at last. At least, the girls did. I'll tell you how it happened.

It was a day in late autumn, and I happened to be over doing some shopping in the little town overlooking the harbour, three miles from this place, and suddenly I saw the old man, the missus, the three girls and Boy all making their way up to Pont—that's at the head of a creek going eastward from the harbour. There are a few cottages at Pont, and a farm and a church up behind. The family looked washed and spruced up, and so did the old man and the missus, and I wondered if they were going visiting. If they were, it was an unusual thing for them to do. But it's possible they had friends or acquaintances up there, of whom I knew nothing. Anyway, that was the last I saw of them, on the fine Saturday afternoon, making for Pont.

It blew hard over the week-end, a proper easterly gale. I

kept indoors and didn't go out at all. I knew the seas would be breaking good and hard on the beach. I wondered if the old man and the family had been able to get back. They would have been wise to stay with their friends up Pont, if they had friends there.

It was Tuesday before the wind dropped and I went down to the beach again. Seaweed, driftwood, tar and oil all over the place. It's always the same after an easterly blow. I looked up the lake, towards the old man's shack, and I saw him there, with the missus, just by the edge of the lake. But there was no sign of the youngsters.

I thought it a bit funny, and waited around in case they should appear. They never did. I walked right round the lake, and from the opposite bank I had a good view of their place, and even took out my old spy-glass to have a closer look. They just weren't there. The old man was pottering about as he often did when he wasn't fishing, and the missus had settled herself down to bask in the sun. There was only one explanation. They had left the family with friends in Pont. They had sent the family for a holiday .

I can't help admitting I was relieved, because for one frightful moment I thought maybe they had started off back home on the Saturday night and got struck by the gale; and, well—that the old man and his missus had got back safely, but not the kids. It couldn't be that, though, I should have heard. Someone would have said something. The old man wouldn't be pottering there in his usual unconcerned fashion and the missus basking in the sun. No, that must have been it. They had left the family with friends. Or maybe the girls and Boy had gone up country, gone to find themselves jobs at last.

Somehow it left a gap. I felt sad. So long now I had been used to seeing them all around. Tiny and the others. I had a strange sort of feeling that they had gone for good. Silly, wasn't it? To mind, I mean. There was the old man, and his missus, and the four youngsters, and I'd more or less watched them grow up, and now for no reason they had gone.

I wished then I knew even a word or two of his language, so that I could have called out to him, neighbour-like, and said, 'I see you and the missus are on your own. Nothing wrong, I hope?'

But there, it wasn't any use. He'd have looked at me with his strange eyes and told me to go to hell.

I never saw the girls again. No, never. They just didn't come back. Once I thought I saw Tiny, somewhere up the estuary, with a group of friends, but I couldn't be sure. If it was, she'd grown, she looked different. I tell you what I think. I think the old man and the missus took them with a definite end in view, that last week-end, and either settled them with friends they knew or told them to shift for themselves.

I know it sounds hard, not what you'd do for your own son and daughters, but you have to remember the old man was a tough customer, a law unto himself. No doubt he thought it would be for the best, and so it probably was, and if only I could know for certain what happened to the girls, especially Tiny, I wouldn't worry.

But I do worry sometimes, because of what happened to Boy. You see, Boy was fool enough to come back. He came back about three weeks after that final week-end. I had walked down through the woods—not my usual way, but down to the lake by the stream that feeds it from a higher level. I rounded the lake by the marshes to the north, some distance from the old man's place, and the first thing I saw was Boy.

He wasn't doing anything. He was just standing by the marsh. He looked dazed. He was too far off for me to hail him; besides, I didn't have the nerve. But I watched him, as he stood there in his clumsy loutish way, and I saw him staring at the far end of the lake. He was staring in the direction of the old man.

The old man, and the missus with him, took not the slightest notice of Boy. They were close to the beach, by the plank bridge, and were either just going out to fish or coming back. And here was Boy, with his dazed stupid face, but not only stupid—frightened.

I wanted to say, 'Is anything the matter?' but I didn't know how to say it. I stood there, like Boy, staring at the old man.

Then what we both must have feared would happen, happened.

The old man lifted his head, and saw Boy.

He must have said a word to his missus, because she didn't move, she stayed where she was, by the bridge, but the old man turned like a flash of lightning and came down the other side of the lake towards the marshes, towards Boy. He looked terrible. I shall never forget his appearance. That magnificent head I had always admired now angry, evil; and he was cursing Boy as he came. I tell you, I heard him.

Boy, bewildered, scared, looked hopelessly about him for cover. There was none. Only the thin reeds that grew beside the marsh. But the poor fellow was so dumb he went in there, and crouched, and believed himself safe—it was a horrible sight.

I was just getting my own courage up to interfere when the old man stopped suddenly in his tracks, pulled up short as it were, and then, still cursing, muttering, turned back again and returned to the bridge. Boy watched him, from his cover of reeds, then, poor clot that he was, came out on to the marsh again, with some idea, I suppose, of striking for home.

I looked about me. There was no one to call. No one to give any help. And if I went and tried to get someone from the farm they would tell me not to interfere, that the old man was best left alone when he got in one of his rages, and anyway that Boy was old enough to take care of himself. He was as big as the old man. He could give as good as he got. I knew different. Boy was no fighter. He didn't know how.

I waited quite a time beside the lake but nothing happened. It began to grow dark. It was no use my waiting there. The old man and the missus left the bridge and went on home. Boy was still standing there on the marsh, by the lake's edge.

I called to him, softly. 'It's no use. He won't let you in. Go back to Pont, or wherever it is you've been. Go to some place, anywhere, but get out of here.'

He looked up, that same queer dazed expression on his face, and I could tell he hadn't understood a word I said.

I felt powerless to do any more. I went home myself. But I thought about Boy all evening, and in the morning I went down to the lake again, and I took a great stick with me to give me courage. Not that it would have been much good. Not against the old man.

Well . . .I suppose they had come to some sort of agreement during the night. There was Boy, by his mother's side, and the old man was pottering on his own.

I must say, it was a great relief. Because, after all, what could I have said or done? If the old man didn't want Boy home, it was really his affair. And if Boy was too stupid to go, that was Boy's affair.

But I blamed the mother a good deal. After all, it was up to her to tell Boy he was in the way, and the old man was in one of his moods, and Boy had best get out while the going was good. But I never did think she had great intelligence. She did not seem to show much spirit at any time.

However, what arrangement they had come to worked for a time. Boy stuck close to his mother—I suppose he helped her at home, I don't know—and the old man left them alone and was more and more by himself.

He took to sitting down by the bridge, humped, staring out to sea, with a queer brooding look on him. He seemed strange, and lonely. I didn't like it. I don't know what his thoughts were, but I'm sure they were evil. It suddenly seemed a very long time since he and the missus and the whole family had gone fishing, a happy, contented party. Now everything had changed for him. He was thrust out in the cold, and the missus and Boy stayed together.

I felt sorry for him, but I felt frightened too. Because I felt it could not go on like this indefinitely; something would happen.

One day I went down to the beach for driftwood—it had been blowing in the night—and when I glanced towards the lake I saw that Boy wasn't with his mother. He was back where I had seen him that first day, on the edge of the marsh. He was as big as his father. If he'd known how to use his strength he'd have been a match for him any day, but he hadn't the brains. There he was, back on the marsh, a great big frightened foolish fellow, and there was the old man, outside his home, staring down towards his son with murder in his eyes.

I said to myself, 'He's going to kill him.' But I didn't know how or when or where, whether by night, when they were sleeping, or by day, when they were fishing. The mother was useless, she would not prevent it. It was no use appealing to the mother. If only Boy would use one little grain of sense, and go. . . .

I watched and waited until nightfall. Nothing happened.

It rained in the night. It was grey, and cold, and dim. December was everywhere, trees all bare and bleak. I couldn't get down to the lake until late afternoon, and then the skies had cleared and the sun was shining in that watery way it does in winter, a burst of it, just before setting below the sea.

I saw the old man, and the missus too. They were close together, by the old shack, and they saw me coming for they looked towards me. Boy wasn't there. He wasn't on the marsh, either. Nor by the side of the lake.

I crossed the bridge and went along the right bank of the lake, and I had my spy-glass with me, but I couldn't see Boy. Yet all the time I was aware of the old man watching me.

Then I saw him. I scrambled down the bank, and crossed the marsh, and went to the thing I saw lying there, behind the reeds.

He was dead. There was a great gash on his body. Dried blood on his back. But he had lain there all night. His body was sodden with the rain.

Maybe you'll think I'm a fool, but I began to cry, like an idiot, and I shouted across to the old man, 'You murderer, you bloody God-damned murderer.' He did not answer. He did not move. He stood there, outside his shack with the missus, watching me.

You'll want to know what I did. I went back and got a spade, and I dug a grave for Boy, in the reeds behind the marsh, and I said one of my own prayers for him, being uncertain of his religion. When I had finished I looked across the lake to the old man.

And do you know what I saw?

I saw him lower his great head, and bend towards her and embrace her. And she lifted her head to him and embraced him too. It was both a requiem and a benediction. An atonement, and a giving of praise. In their strange way they knew they had done evil, but now it was over, because I had buried Boy and he was gone. They were free to be together again, and there was no longer a third to divide them.

They came out into the middle of the lake, and suddenly I saw the old man stretch his neck and beat his wings, and he took off from the water, full of power, and she followed him. I watched the two swans fly out to sea right into the face of the setting sun, and I tell you it was one of the most beautiful sights I ever saw in my life: the two swans flying there, alone, in winter.

John Wyndham

JOHN WYNDHAM, like Evelyn Waugh, was born in 1903. Like Evelyn Waugh, he, too, wrote his first book when he was twenty-two.

For many years he wrote stories of various kinds under different names for American magazines. At the same time he tried several careers, including farming, law, commercial art and advertising.

Later he wrote detective novels, and then he tried his hand at science-fiction. He was an almost immediate success. His books such as *The Day of the Triffids* and *The Kraken Wakes* have been translated into many languages, and have been adapted for broadcasting.

COMPASSION CIRCUIT

BY THE time Janet had been five days in hospital she had become converted to the idea of a domestic robot. It had taken her two days to discover that Nurse James *was* a robot, one day to get over the surprise, and two more to realize what a comfort an attendant robot could be.

The conversion was a relief. Practically every house she visited had a domestic robot; it was the family's second or third most valuable possession—the women tended to rate it slightly higher than the car; the men, slightly lower. Janet had been perfectly well aware for some time that her friends regarded her as a nitwit or worse for wearing herself out with looking after a house which a robot would be able to keep spick and span with a few hours' work a day. She had also known that it irritated George to come home each evening to a wife who had tired herself out by unnecessary work. But the prejudice had been firmly set. It was not the diehard attitude of people who refused to be served by robot waiters, or driven by robot drivers (who, incidentally were much safer), led by robot shop guides, or see dresses modelled by robot mannequins. It was simply an uneasiness about them, and being left alone with one —and a disinclination to feel such an uneasiness in her own home.

She herself attributed the feeling largely to the conservatism of her own home which had used no house-robots. Other people, who had been brought up in homes run by robots, even the primitive types available a generation before, never seemed to have such a feeling at all. It irritated her to know that her husband thought she was *afraid* of them in a childish way. That, she had explained to George a number of times, was not so, and was not the point, either: what she did dislike was the idea of one intruding upon her personal, domestic life, which was what a house-robot was bound to do.

The robot who was called Nurse James was, then, the first with which she had ever been in close personal contact and she, or it, came as a revelation.

Janet told the doctor of her enlightenment, and he looked relieved. She also told George when he looked in in the afternoon: he was delighted. The two of them conferred before he left the hospital. 'Excellent,' said the doctor. 'To tell you the truth I was afraid we were up against a real neurosis there—and very inconveniently too. Your wife can never have been strong, and in the last few years she has worn herself out running the house.'

'I know,' George agreed. 'I tried hard to persuade her during the first two years we were married, but it only led to trouble so I had to drop it. This is really a culmination—she was rather shaken when she found that the reason she'd have to come here was partly because there was no robot at home to look after her.'

'Well, there's one thing certain, she can't go on as she has been doing. If she tries to she'll be back here inside a couple of months,' the doctor told him.

'She won't now. She's really changed her mind,' George assured him. 'Part of the trouble was that she's never come across a really modern one, except in a superficial way. The newest that any of our friends has is ten years old at least, and most of them are older than that. She'd never contemplated the idea of anything as advanced as Nurse James. The question now is what pattern?'

The doctor thought a moment. 'Frankly, Mr. Shand, your wife is going to need a lot of rest and looking after, I'm afraid. What I'd really recommend for her is the type they have here. It's something pretty new this Nurse James model. A specially developed high-sensibility job with a quite novel contra-balanced compassion-protection circuit—a very tricky bit of work that—any direct order which a normal robot would obey at once is evaluated by the circuit, it is weighed against the benefit or harm to the patient, and unless it is beneficial, or at least harmless, to the patient, it is not obeyed. They've proved to be wonderful for nursing and looking after children—but there is big demand for them, and I'm afraid they're pretty expensive.'

'How much?' asked George.

The doctor's round-figure price made him frown for a moment. Then he said:

'It'll make a hole, but, after all, it's mostly Janet's economies and simple living that's built up the savings. Where do I get one?'

'You don't. Not just like that,' the doctor told him. 'I shall have to throw a lot of weight about for a priority, but in the circumstances I shall get it, all right. Now, you go and fix up the details of appearance and so on with your wife. Let me know how she wants it, and I'll get busy.'

'A proper one,' said Janet. 'One that'll look right in a house, I mean. I couldn't do with one of those levers-and-plastic-box things that stare at you with lenses. As it's got to look after the house, let's have it looking like a housemaid.'

'Or a houseman, if you like?'

She shook her head. 'No. It's going to have to look after me, too, so I think I'd rather it was rather a housemaid. It can have a black silk dress and a frilly white apron and a cap. And I'd like it blonde—a sort of darkish blonde—and about five feet ten, and nice to look at, but not too beautiful. I don't want to be jealous of it. . . .'

The doctor kept Janet ten days more in the hospital while the matter was settled. There had been luck in coming in for a cancelled order, but inevitably some delay while it was adapted to Janet's specifications—also it had required the addition of standard domestic, pseudo-memory patterns to suit it for housework.

It was delivered the day after she got back. Two severely functional robots carried the case up the front path, and inquired whether they should unpack it. Janet thought not, and told them to leave it in the outhouse.

When George got back he wanted to open it at once, but Janet shook her head.

'Supper first,' she decided. 'A robot doesn't mind waiting.'

Nevertheless it was a brief meal. When it was over, George carried the dishes out and stacked them in the sink.

'No more washing-up,' he said, with satisfaction.

He went out to borrow the next door robot to help him carry the case in. Then he found his end of it more than he could lift, and had to borrow the robot from the house opposite, too. Presently the pair of them carried it in and laid it on the kitchen floor as if it were a featherweight, and went away again.

George got out the screwdriver and drew the six large screws that held the lid down. Inside was a mass of shavings, he shoved them out on the floor.

Janet protested.

'What's the matter? We shan't have to clear up,' he said, happily.

There was an inner case of wood pulp, with a snowy layer of wadding under its lid. George rolled it up and pushed it out of the way, and there, ready dressed in black frock and white apron, lay the robot.

They regarded it for some seconds without speaking.

It was remarkably lifelike. For some reason it made Janet feel a little queer to realize that it was her robot—a trifle nervous, and, obscurely, a trifle guilty. . . .

'Sleeping Beauty,' remarked George, reaching for the instruction book on its chest.

In point of fact the robot was not a beauty. Janet's preference had been observed. It was pleasant and nice-looking without being striking, but the details were good. The deep gold hair was quite enviable—although one knew that it was probably threads of plastic with waves that would never come out. The skin—another kind of plastic covering the carefully built-up contours—was distinguishable from real skin only by its perfection.

Janet knelt down beside the box, and ventured a forefinger to touch the flawless complexion. It was quite, quite cold.

She sat back on her heels, looking at it. Just a big doll, she told herself; a contraption, a very wonderful contraption of metal, plastics, and electronic circuits, but still a contraption, and made to look as it did simply because people, including herself, would find it harsh or grotesque if it should look any other way. . . . And yet, to have it looking as it did was a bit disturbing, too. For one thing, you couldn't go on thinking of it as 'it' any more; whether you liked it or not, your mind thought of it as 'her'. As 'her' it would have to have a name; and, with a name, it would become still more of a person.

' "A battery-driven model," ' George read out, ' "will normally require to be fitted with a new battery every four days. Other models, however, are designed to conduct their own regeneration from the mains as and when necessary." Let's have her out.'

He put his hands under the robot's shoulders, and tried to lift it.

'Phew!' he said. 'Must be about three times my weight.' He had another try. 'Hell,' he said, and referred to the book again. ' "The control switches are situated at the back, slightly above the waistline." All right, maybe we can roll her over.'

With an effort he succeeded in getting the figure on to its side and began to undo the buttons at the back of her dress. Janet suddenly felt that to be an indelicacy.

'I'll do it,' she said.

Her husband glanced at her.

'All right. It's yours,' he told her.

'She can't be just "it". I'm going to call her Hester.'

'All right, again,' he agreed.

Janet undid the buttons and fumbled about inside the dress. 'I can't find a knob, or anything,' she said.

'Apparently there's a small panel that opens,' he told her.

'Oh, no!' she said, in a slightly shocked tone.

He regarded her again. 'Darling, she's just a robot; a mechanism.'

'I know,' said Janet shortly. She felt about again, discovered the panel, and opened it.

'You give the upper knob a half-turn to the right and then

close the panel to complete the circuit,' instructed George, from the book.

Janet did so, and then sat swiftly back on her heels again, watching.

The robot stirred and turned. It sat up, then it got to its feet. It stood before them, looking the very pattern of a stage parlourmaid.

'Good day, madam,' it said. 'Good day, sir. I shall be happy to serve you.'

'Thank you, Hester,' Janet said, as she leaned back against the cushion placed behind her. Not that it was necessary to thank a robot, but she had a theory that if you did not practise politeness with robots you soon forgot it with other people.

And, anyway, Hester was no ordinary robot. She was not even dressed as a parlourmaid any more. In four months she had become a friend, a tireless, attentive friend. From the first Janet had found it difficult to believe that she was only a mechanism, and as the days passed she had become more and more of a person. The fact that she consumed electricity instead of food came to seem little more than a foible. The time she couldn't stop walking in a circle, and the other time when something went wrong with her vision so that she did everything a foot to the right of where she ought to have been doing it, these things were just indispositions such as anyone might have, and the robot-mechanic who came to adjust her paid his call much like any other doctor. Hester was not only a person; she was preferable company to many.

'I suppose,' said Janet, settling back in her chair, 'that you must think me a poor, weak thing?'

What one must not expect from Hester was euphemism. 'Yes,' she said, directly. But then she added: 'I think all humans are poor, weak things. It is the way they are made. One must be sorry for them.'

Janet had long ago given up thinking things like: 'That'll be the compassion-circuit speaking,' or trying to imagine the computing, selecting, associating, and shunting that must be going on to produce such a remark. She took it as she might from—well, say, a foreigner. She said:

'Compared with robots we must seem so, I suppose. You are so strong and untiring, Hester. If you knew how I envy you that. . . .'

Hester said, matter of factly:

'We were designed: you were just accidental. It is your misfortune, not your fault.'

'You'd rather be you than me?' asked Janet.

'Certainly,' Hester told her. 'We are stronger. We don't have to have frequent sleep to recuperate. We don't have to carry an unreliable chemical factory inside us. We don't have to grow old and deteriorate. Human beings are so clumsy and fragile and so often unwell because something is not working properly. If anything goes wrong with us, or is broken, it doesn't hurt and is easily replaced. And you have all kinds of words like pain and suffering, and unhappiness, and weariness that we have to be taught to understand, and they don't seem to us to be useful things to have. I feel very sorry that you must have these things and be so uncertain and so fragile. It disturbs my compassion-circuit.'

'Uncertain and fragile,' Janet repeated. 'Yes, that's how I feel.'

'Humans have to live so precariously,' Hester went on. 'If my arm or leg should be crushed I can have a new one in a few minutes, but a human would have agony for a long time, and not even a new limb at the end of it—just a faulty one, if he is lucky. That isn't as bad as it used to be because in designing us you learned how to make good arms and legs, much stronger and better than the old ones. People would be much more sensible to have a weak arm or leg replaced at once, but they don't seem to want to if they can possibly keep the old ones.'

'You mean they can be grafted on? I didn't know that,' Janet said. 'I wish it were only arms or legs that's wrong with me. I don't think I would hesitate. . . .' She sighed. 'The doctor wasn't encouraging this morning, Hester. You heard what he said? I've been losing ground: must rest more. I don't believe he does expect me to get any stronger. He was just trying to cheer me up before. . . . He had a funny sort of look after he examined me. . . . But all he said was rest. What's the good of being alive if it's only rest—rest—rest . . .? And there's poor George. What sort of life is it for him, and he's so patient with me, so sweet. . . . I'd rather anything than go on feebly like this. I'd sooner die. . . .'

Janet went on talking, more to herself than to the patient Hester standing by. She talked herself into tears. Then, presently she looked up.

'Oh, Hester, if you were human I couldn't bear it; I think I'd hate you for being so strong and well—but I don't, Hester. You're so kind and so patient when I'm silly, like this. I believe you'd cry with me to keep me company if you could.'

'I would if I could,' the robot agreed. 'My compassion-circuit——'

'Oh, no!' Janet protested. 'It can't be just that. You've a heart somewhere, Hester. You must have.'

'I expect it is more reliable than a heart,' said Hester.

She stepped a little closer, stooped down, and lifted Janet up as if she weighed nothing at all.

'You've tired yourself out, Janet, dear,' she told her. 'I'll take you upstairs; you'll be able to sleep a little before he gets back.'

Janet could feel the robot's arms cold through her dress, but the coldness did not trouble her any more, she was aware only that they were strong, protecting arms around her. She said:

'Oh, Hester, you are such a comfort, you *know* what I ought to do.' She paused, then she added miserably: 'I know what he thinks—the doctor, I mean. I could see it. He just thinks I am going to go on getting weaker and weaker until one day I'll fade away and die. . . . I said I'd sooner die . . . but I wouldn't, Hester. I don't want to die. . . .'

The robot rocked her a little, as if she were a child.

'There, there, dear. It's not as bad as that—nothing like,' she told her. 'You mustn't think about dying. And you mustn't cry any more, it's not good for you, you know. Besides, you don't want him to see you've been crying.'

'I'll try not to,' agreed Janet obediently, as Hester carried her out of the room and up the stairs.

The hospital reception-robot looked up from the desk. 'My wife,' George said, 'I rang you up about an hour ago.'

The robot's face took on an impeccable expression of professional sympathy.

'Yes, Mr. Shand, I'm afraid it has been a shock for you, but as I told you, your house-robot did the right thing to send her here at once.'

'I've tried to get on to her own doctor, but he's away,' George told her.

'You don't need to worry about that, Mr. Shand. She has been examined, and we have had all her records sent over from the hospital she was in before. The operation has been provisionally fixed for tomorrow, but of course we shall need your consent.'

George hesitated. 'May I see the doctor in charge of her?'

'He isn't in the hospital at the moment, I'm afraid.'

'Is it—absolutely necessary?' George asked after a pause.

The robot looked at him steadily and nodded. 'She must have been growing steadily weaker for some months now,' she said.

George nodded.

'The only alternative is that she will grow weaker still, and have more pain before the end,' she told him.

George stared blankly at the wall for some seconds. 'I see,' he said bleakly.

He picked up a pen in a shaky hand and signed the form that she put before him. He gazed at it a while without seeing it.

'She'll—she'll have—a good chance?' he asked.

'Yes,' the robot told him. 'There is never complete absence of risk, of course, but she has a better than seventy-per-cent likelihood of complete success.'

George sighed, and nodded. 'I'd like to see her,' he said.

The robot pressed a bell-push. 'You may see her,' she said. 'But I must ask you not to disturb her. She's asleep now, and it's better for her not to be woken.'

George had to be satisfied with that, but he left the hospital feeling a little better for the sight of the quiet smile on Janet's lips as she slept.

The hospital called him at the office the following afternoon. They were reassuring. The operation appeared to have been a complete success. Everyone was quite confident of the outcome. There was no need to worry. The doctors were perfectly satisfied. No, it would not be wise to allow any visitors for a few days yet. But there was nothing to worry about. Nothing at all.

George rang up each day just before he left, in the hope that he would be allowed a visit. The hospital was kindly and heartening, but adamant about visits. And then, on the fifth day, they suddenly told him she had left on her way home.

George was staggered: he had been prepared to find it a matter of weeks. He dashed out, bought a bunch of roses, and left half a dozen traffic regulations in fragments behind him.

'Where is she?' he demanded of Hester as she opened the door.

'She's in bed. I thought it might be better if—' Hester began, but he lost the rest of the sentence as he bounded up the stairs.

Janet was lying in the bed. Only her head was visible, cut off by the line of the sheet and a bandage round her neck. George put the flowers down on the bedside table. He stooped over Janet, and kissed her gently. She looked up at him from anxious eyes.

'Oh, George dear. Has she told you?'

'Has who told me what?' he asked, sitting down on the side of the bed.

'Hester. She said she would. Oh, George, I didn't mean it, at least I don't think I meant it. . . . She sent me, George. I was so weak and wretched. I wanted to be strong. I don't think I really understood. Hester said——'

'Take it easy, darling. Take it easy,' George suggested with a smile. 'What on earth's all this about?'

He felt under the bedclothes and found her hand.

'But, George——' she began. He interrupted her.

'I say, darling, your hand's dreadfully cold. It's almost like——' His fingers slid further up her arm. His eyes widened at her, incredulously. He jumped up suddenly from the bed and flung back the covers. He put his hand on the thin night-dress over her heart—and then snatched it away as if he had been stung.

'God!—NO!—' he said, staring at her.

'But George. George, darling——' said Janet's head on the pillows.

'NO!—*NO!*' cried George, almost in a shriek.

He turned and ran blindly from the room.

In the darkness on the landing he missed the top step of the stairs, and went headlong down the whole flight.

Hester found him lying in a muddle in the hall. She bent down and gently explored the damage. The extent of it, and the fragility of the frame that had suffered it disturbed her compassion-circuit very greatly. She did not try to move him, but went to the telephone and dialled.

'Emergency?' she asked, and gave the name and address. 'Yes, at once,' she told them. 'There may not be a lot of time. Several compound fractures, and I think his back is broken, poor man. No. There appears to be no damage to his head. Yes, much better. He'd be crippled for life, even if he did get over it. . . . Yes, better send the form of consent with the ambulance so that it can be signed at once. . . . Oh yes, that'll be quite all right. His wife will sign it.'

H. E. Bates

H. E. BATES, who attended Kettering Grammar School, had his first book published when he was in his early twenties.

Since then he has written more than forty books. His work has been translated into fifteen languages and has been used in school editions in many countries, among them Japan.

During the war Bates served in the Far East with the R.A.F., and wrote short stories under the pseudonym of Flying Officer 'X'.

He now lives in Kent where he divides his time between gardening—growing orchids—and what he calls his whole time recreation —writing itself. He confesses to never being really happy except when writing.

Bates has four children, two sons and two daughters, says he loves football and hates men's clubs.

He is one of our leading writers of the short story, and his best works often suggest the effects of poetry.

THE DIAMOND HAIR-PIN

FOR SOME weeks after he had first found the hair-pin on the wooden seat in the park Tom Wakeling kept it wrapped up in tissue paper in a table drawer at his lodgings. It was a perfectly ordinary hair-pin, though perhaps rather longer than usual, except that it carried with it, for a time, a strong scent of carnations.

A few strands of dark hair were still clinging to it when he first picked it up and it was they, together with the scent of carnations, that made him start wondering, at first casually and then so deeply that it became an obsession, what sort of woman had left it there.

Soon he was going back to sit on the same park seat every

evening after his work in the drawing office was over. The seat was on the bank of a small lake where flocks of mallard, various other ornamental ducks, a few swan-necked geese, and occasional sea-gulls fought and dived for scraps of food thrown in by visitors.

He liked to throw pieces of bread to the birds himself and as he sat there breaking it up in his fingers he also looked very ordinary: shy, scrubby-haired, his skin rather pasty, his eyes seemingly short-focused, as if from long hours of concentration over the drawing board. His hands were in fact the only features about him that were at all unusual. The fingers were long and narrow and very white. Because of his work they were immaculately kept, every inch of them so unblemished that they too, like the hair-pin, might have been wrapped up at night in tissue paper and carefully laid away.

The obsession with the hair-pin got hold of him slowly but, having taken hold, soon had him locked in hopeless entrancement. A more communicative type of person might have told himself that girls didn't wear hair-pins like that any longer. Old ladies did, however, and it therefore naturally followed that nobody more exciting than an old lady throwing bread to the ducks could have lost the pin—it simply wasn't worth bothering about anyway.

But a mind as cautious, withdrawn and self-centred as his couldn't relinquish facts so easily. Just as he drew lines on a sheet of paper with minutest accuracy so he microscopically scrutinized the facts. And the facts were that old ladies didn't have black hair and, unless he was much mistaken, didn't use the scent of carnations either. It seemed patently obvious to him that an altogether younger, more exciting, and possibly provocative person had dropped the pin from her hair.

It was after nearly a month of this cautious and earnest speculation that the impossibly idiotic notion of advertising the hair-pin in a newspaper first came to him—except that to his sort of mind the idea seemed neither idiotic nor impossible. When he came to measure the facts it was clearly no more unusual than four-fifths of the things people expounded in the personal columns of newspapers every day—the heart cries for loved ones to come home, the pleas for stray cats, pet mice, and budgerigars to be returned to their heart-broken owners, the rewards offered for the recovery of lost trifles, the universal promise that, at last, all was forgiven.

But when he came to frame the advertisement—he would put it in an evening paper, he thought, it was the sort of thing that might catch the eye of a girl going home on a bus or train —it wasn't so easy. He had to admit that *Found: one black hair-pin. Owner please communicate Box No. X* sounded pretty pointless. The only possible explanation a lot of people would find for it was that it was a message in some sort of code. It might be anything from an agreed signal between crooks that a bank was ripe for picking or a communication of immense secrecy between lovers.

Whatever interpretation people might put on it he was perfectly sure that he would get numbers of useless and stupid replies. And he didn't want that; he was perfectly serious about it all. He had even built up in the more cautious recesses of his mind an image of the sort of girl who had lost the pin. To him there was nothing strange about that; nor was there anything strange in nursing the hope that one day, somewhere, some-how, in some miraculous sort of way, he might meet her. A delightful experience might come out of it.

Even so he grasped the necessity of making his advertise-ment more specific and, if possible, more tempting. And finally he made it so and put it in the evening paper.

Found: Adelaide Park: evening of June 26: one diamond hair-pin. Owner please communicate earliest possible Box No. X.

He got only three replies. One was from a lady, clearly elderly and acidly irate, who reminded him tersely of the penalties of stealing by finding and why hadn't he advertised before? She didn't claim the pin. The second was from a firm of city jewellers who said that in their experience diamond hair-pins were of such rarity that they would consider it a great favour if they might have the privilege of inspecting this one.

The third was from a person named Aimée Vibert. She wrote to him in rather laboured, long-lettered script on dark blue paper. She too, he thought, was evidently living in lodgings, since her address was c/o Miss A. Winter. She wrote:

'You do not describe the pin with any detail but I myself am sure it is the one I lost six months ago and have never seen since. It was given to me by my aunt for my fifteenth birthday just before the war.'

He was pleased about this letter, which he read over and over again before deciding how to answer it. It not only told him that his correspondent had an elegant-sounding, rather exciting foreign name, but also roughly how old she was. His calculations put her at thirty-five or thirty-six, a year or two younger than he was. He eventually wrote back:

'If you could spare the time to meet me I would be happy to bring the pin along so that you can identify it. Would it suit you to meet me in the park, say at 7 o'clock on Thursday, at the seat where I found the pin? It is the third seat along from the little kiosk on the north side of the lake. I shall be wearing a grey charcoal suit and in all probability will be carrying a paper bag of bread which I shall bring for the birds.'

She replied to this, on the same kind of unusually dark blue paper:

'I am afraid I am not able to manage to meet you earlier than half-past seven, as my companion, Miss Winter, likes us to eat at half-past six. Otherwise I look forward to meeting you and making your acquaintance. Please don't forget the pin. It is rather precious to me.'

After he had read this second letter several times he suddenly held it to his nose, sniffing it in the hope of smelling carnations, but the paper gave off no scent of anything at all.

Half an hour before he was due to meet her rain began to fall in the lightest of summer showers. The fragrance of rain on dust filled the park as he walked across it under an umbrella, carrying the paper bag of scraps of bread and biscuit which he had saved from his tea.

Although the rain stopped a few minutes before half past seven the park seat was wet, so that he couldn't sit down. Instead he rolled up his umbrella, leaned on it at the edge of the lake and started to feed the ducks with scraps of food. He seemed to do this with an air of great casualness, though in reality the palms of his long hands were as wet as if he had held them out in the rain.

At a quarter to eight she was standing there beside him and he was sure at once that she was foreign. She had straight light brown hair cut short and a sallow complexion that made her look as if she had been shut away somewhere for a long time. She was extremely plain but an extraordinary transparency in the eyes gave them a brilliance that made up for all lack of colour. She was astonishingly thin too and was wearing one of those stone-grey mackintoshes that have shoulder flaps that protrude like ears, so that it looked several sizes too large for her.

'I'm Tom Wakeling. I suppose you could be the lady who has come about the hair-pin?'

'Yes. That is so.' She spoke very formally, in a hopeless sort of voice, with a marked accent. 'Good evening.'

'Good evening.'

He instinctively made as if to shake hands but succeeded only in rattling the scraps of food in the paper bag.

'I'm sorry it rained,' he said.

'I am sorry, too.'

'I'm afraid it's made the seats wet.'

'I'm afraid it has.'

'I think the kiosk is still open. Perhaps we could sit there.'

'Perhaps we could.'

'They have fairly good coffee.' He threw a few desperate scraps of food into the lake. The ducks, mostly mallards, fanned about them madly and from across the water three gulls swept like pairs of flying scissors. 'Would you like some coffee?'

'I think it may be a good idea. Thank you.'

The seats at the kiosk were under indigo blue umbrellas and had kept dry. The colour of the umbrellas reminded him of the notepaper she used. In some extraordinary way the diffusion of it in the rather dull evening air made her face seem to shrink and become plainer and thinner than ever.

While waiting for the coffee to arrive he said several times that he hoped it wouldn't rain again. She said she hoped so too. He said, several times also, that he liked feeding the ducks. It was his favourite place along here, even in winter. He was always coming here. It whiled away the time.

All the time he was dreading the moment when she would ask about the pin, which he hadn't brought with him and never would, and as soon as the coffee arrived he passed the sugar to her and said in an effort to be casual:

'Where are you from?'

'I am from Austria.'

'Ah! Vienna. I have never been there.'

'I am from near Linz. Not Vienna.'

'Have you been in England long?'

'Nearly one year.'

The evening sun was actually breaking through the clouds by now, making the vapour rise from the lake edge. The ducks were paddling about in a light cloud of steam and as he watched them he started to ponder on the name Vibert. It sounded rather more French than German, he thought.

'Do you pronounce Vibert to rhyme with *bear* or with *hurt*?' he said.

Perhaps it was the very clumsiness or silliness of this that made her seem suddenly ill-at-ease. She didn't answer for some seconds and he said:

'I only asked because it seemed rather like a French name.'

'Oh! yes. That is so. My father was French. His mother was named Aimée.'

Slowly sipping his coffee, he started to have fresh thoughts about the name.

'In a funny sort of way,' he said, 'I seem to have heard your name before.'

'Sometimes it is happening like that.'

'Aimée Vibert,' he started to say, 'it sort of——'

'Truly speaking my father was not really French. He came to Austria as a boy. He was brought up there. He even could hardly speak French.'

Most of the time she fixed a hopeless stare on the lake, more than half hiding her face every time she lifted the coffee cup to it with both hands. He was still too shy to watch her very closely but whenever he did so he felt the once provocative image of a dark-haired woman carrying the scent of carnations in her hair grow fainter and fainter.

After an especially long silence he once again became scared that she would ask about the pin and he said:

'What do you do?'

'I hope to be a children's nurse.'

'Hope? Is it so difficult?'

'To find the right family is difficult. I myself am from a good family.'

'So naturally——'

'Naturally. After all it is not in every family that the mother gives her daughter a diamond hair-pin for a birthday——'

He felt his insides turn sick and sour at this pointed mention of the pin but even in this spasm of physical misery he managed to say:

'I thought it was your aunt gave it to you?'

'Yes: that is so. My mother gave me one and my aunt the other. They were a pair, you see.'

'I see. Would you like some more coffee?'

'I think so. Please.'

After he had fetched fresh cups of coffee from the kiosk he felt his dread about the pin increasing. At the same time he was whipped by curiosity to know what her own pin looked like and if she had brought it with her.

'No. I have not brought it this time.'

'Why not?'

'I felt I had to see what you were like first.'

He felt himself violently sweating again. At the same time a gull rode stridently across the lake, a fish in its mouth, screamingly pursued by two others diving in battle. He looked up and actually saw a pink fin, like a rosy arrowhead, sticking out of the long gull's beak before the two darting pursuers drove it away across the water.

'There's a battle for you. Do you find the birds exciting?'

'I really don't know.' Her voice sounded flat and monotonous. 'I hadn't thought about it.'

'I do. I'm always here watching them. You never know what you'll see. Like that fight, I mean.'

'You come alone?'

'Mostly.'

'Haven't you any friends?'

'Not really.'

His excruciating shyness seemed to snap a pair of clips across the lids of his eyes. He felt his eyeballs stiffen defensively as she tried to probe out yet another detail of his life:

'You live alone?'

'Oh! yes.'

And then, as he sat transfixed as a butterfly on a pin, she stirred rapidly at her coffee and said:

'Did you bring the pin with you?'

'Well——'

For a few desperate minutes he resisted new agonies, finally pulled himself together and managed to frame a line or two he had rehearsed for most of the day:

'No, I didn't actually. It's being repaired. One of the diamonds became loose and dropped out. It'll take a day or two——'

'Is it the one at the top? You know, where the bend is?'

'Yes,' he said, 'that's the one.'

'It was always coming out,' she said.

He sat in the big silent trap of his own making, head down, utterly at a loss for anything to say. When after some time he looked up again he saw her completely engrossed in a dark stare across the lake. She might have been casting her mind back to a troubled incident of some sort and it made him say:

'Is Austria nice? What is it like in Austria?'

Without any hesitation at all she said: 'In winter there are great snows.'

'Ah! yes, I suppose so.'

'Sometimes they drifted many metres up the walls of the *Schloss*.'

'*Schloss?*'

'The castle. Where I worked.'

The pronounciation of the word 'worked' was so strange that it might well have been 'walked' but he had no time to ponder on this before she said hastily:

'Where I lived I mean.'

'A big castle?'

'Austria is full of castles. There are castles everywhere.'

'I should like to go there once,' he said. 'But not in winter. I feel the cold a great deal and I don't like snow.'

'No? It is very beautiful.'

'I prefer summer. When I think of castles I think of big pine-trees and roses growing over the walls and——'

'Roses? What makes you think of roses?'

'I've no idea,' he said.

Another imponderable silence fell between them like a cloud. On the edge of the lake a quarrel feathered up between a pigeon and a gull. There was a steely smacking of wings and a string of snarls from the gull's beak. Farther out a duck stood on its head, orange feet clawing the air like the hands of a drowning swimmer.

Merely for something to say he asked:

'Is your companion from Austria too?'

'My companion?'

'Miss Winter, isn't that her name?'

'Oh! Anna. I didn't quite catch, she is from Austria too.'

'Is she older than you?'

'Oh! no. She is the same age. The same age exactly.'

Once again the conversation broke down. Shyness drew down the inevitable cloud under which she stared at the lake and in which he separated golden grains of sugar at the bottom of his cup with a coffee spoon.

A sudden squawk from a gull had the effect of starting off his mind in a complete revolution. He was abruptly conscious of a marked click! in his brain, like that of a lens in a camera being set, and it made him jerk out a single word.

'Roses,' he said.

'Please. What did you say?'

The incredible plainness of her face, darkly stained by the blue of the umbrella overhead made the sharp turn of her head excruciatingly painful. It was now as if she too had been caught in a trap.

There was a rose, he had suddenly recalled, named Aimée Vibert. It was an old one, pure white, and his grandfather had grown it on a wall. The link connecting that wall with the *Schloss* far away on some Austrian mountainside whipped itself into a noose that tautened around his throat and he hardly heard her say:

'I didn't quite catch what you said again.'

'I was wondering if you would like some more coffee, that's all.'

'I think I would, please.'

He again picked up the empty coffee cups and took them back to the kiosk. A woman polishing a glass behind a counter said: 'Just in time, dear. Closing down in five minutes,' and filled up the two cups with milky coffee again. He paid for them, took his change, picked up the cups and started to walk back to the table, his hands trembling.

'I was just in time. They'll soon be closing.'

'Yes, it's getting late.'

For some time he had had a growing suspicion that, just as there was no pin, there was no *Schloss*, no companion, no aunt either: nothing but the plain dull face, its hopeless stare and the straight short hair where no hair-pin could ever possibly have sat. The diamond had never fallen from the crest of the pin. There was no Aimée Vibert and the romantic image of a dark-haired woman with a scent of carnations in her hair now sat away in a far corner somewhere, a ghost of a cooled imagination.

'I was wondering,' he said. He stirred his coffee with laborious, thoughtful strokes of the spoon. 'Will you be going back to Austria?'

'I don't think so. At least not for some time.'

'I see.'

'There is plenty of time for the pin if that is what you are thinking.'

'Oh! yes, it will be some time yet.'

The sudden mention of the pin after such a long interval unnerved him again. He gulped at his coffee quickly and then said:

'What made you leave Austria? I mean if you like it and it's so beautiful?'

She looked slowly across the lake, her stare darker again.

'You are interested in that?'

'I'm sorry. I didn't mean to intrude.'

She picked up her coffee spoon and balanced it on the edge of the cup. The bowl floated for a fraction of a second and then sank.

'I wanted to get away from myself. I was in a little trouble there.'

He could find nothing to say to this and laboriously sipped his coffee, not looking at her.

'A friend of mine was killed.'

'I'm sorry.'

'It's strange I should talk to you about it. When I don't wish to remember it.'

'There's no need to talk.'

'I haven't talked to anyone about it for one year.'

For the first time his clumsy deceit about the hair-pin struck him as impossible and painfully idiotic; he felt suddenly cramped with shame.

'It was just an accident.'

'I see.'

'But it looked perhaps that I was responsible.'

Again he had nothing to say. In the last ten minutes the light across the lake had faded perceptibly and on the far side a floating pair of gulls shone like ghosts too.

'It was something that began as a joke and then——'

'A man?'

She paused for some moments and then said:

'No, a girl. We worked at the *Schloss* together.'

This time there was no mistaking the word, it was worked, not walked.

'It's really a hotel.'

So he was right, he thought. She had made it all up. Like the pin—

'I was very fond of her. I did a stupid thing to make her jealous. Just a little stupid thing.'

That was all. The picture, incomplete though it was, flared up before him with a brief white brilliance and then darkened again. He got up. For a moment he didn't want to know any more. The idiotic deceit about the pin gnawed at him like a persistent rat and he drew his long fingers across his face several times as if forcing it away.

'You are going now?' she said.

'I think so. If you are ready.'

She got up too and then, without looking at her, he said:

'Before we go would you mind if I asked you something?'

'Please?'

'I suppose you know there is a rose named Aimée Vibert?'

'Yes,' she said. She had come across it in a magazine; she had

done it on the spur of the moment; it was because she didn't
want to use her proper name.

There was a break in her voice, not so much apologetic as an
invitation for him to say something, to tell her perhaps that
he understood her feelings and her motives about it all. He
knew that the moment had come when he had to say he understood and to tell her too that everything about the pin was a
fake. It was all false; he was a fake too. He had cheated in the
hope of acquiring the experience of something romantic and
all he had got was that plain dark face with its hopeless stare
and now there was no hope of explaining it all. He simply said:

'My grandfather grew that rose. That's how I knew about it.'

She didn't speak. They started to walk slowly along the
lake-side. In a vacuum of indecision he stared ahead, watching
the street lights come on beyond the park. The yellow rays of
them, like strong moonlight, struck upwards into the leaves
of the street-trees, miraculously heightening the pattern of
colours, shapes and veins.

'My name is really Anna Winters,' she said and the voice
was so low that he hardly caught the rest. 'Now you know all
about me.'

Through sudden humiliation at what she had said he made an
abrupt and incredible conquest of shyness. He actually looked
her in the face and said:

'Would you mind if I walked home with you?'

'I would not mind.'

They walked slowly on and once, as they stopped before
crossing the road, he held her back from the passing traffic by
catching at one of the impossible shoulder flaps of her mackintosh. She turned and looked up at him, the immensely trans-
parent eyes quite still under the street-lights. He didn't speak.

'Yes?' she said. 'I thought you were going to say something.'

He was moved yet again to a sudden confession about the

hair-pin and then, instead, heard himself incredibly utter the words:

'Perhaps I could see you tomorrow.'

'If you would like it.'

'The pin won't be ready of course. These things take time.'

'Everything takes time.'

He guided her across the road, still holding the flaps of the mackintosh. He had nothing much more to say. He had said for the time being all he had the courage to say but every now and then, as they walked on in silence, it seemed to him that the face beside him was plain no longer.

L. P. Hartley

LESLIE POLES HARTLEY is a bachelor who lives near Bath in Somerset. He leads an active and busy life, dividing his time between writing his own books and reviewing other people's. At various times he has been literary critic for the *Spectator*, the *Sketch*, and *Time and Tide*.

In addition to two collections of short stories, L. P. Hartley has written several novels, one of which won the James Tait Black Memorial Prize in 1947.

Hartley is fond of the outdoors, and spends much of his spare time by the river, or going for long walks in the country. He was born in 1895, and was educated at Harrow and Balliol College, Oxford.

A HIGH DIVE

THE CIRCUS-MANAGER was worried. Attendances had been falling off and such people as did come—children they were, mostly—sat about listlessly, munching sweets or sucking ices, sometimes talking to each other without so much as glancing at the show. Only the young or little girls, who came to see the ponies, betrayed any real interest. The clowns' jokes fell flat, for they were the kind of jokes that used to raise a laugh before 1939, after which critical date people's sense of humour seemed to have changed, along with many other things about them. The circus-manager had heard the word 'corny' flung about and didn't like it. What did they want? Something that was, in his opinion, sillier and more pointless than the old jokes; not a bull's-eye on the target of humour, but an outer or even a near-miss—something that brought in the element of futility and that could be laughed at as well as with: an unintentional joke against the joker. The clowns were quick enough with their patter but it just didn't go down: there was too much sense in their nonsense for an up-to-date audience, too much articulateness. They would do better to talk gibberish, perhaps. Now they must change their style, and find out what really did make people laugh, if people could be made to; but he, the manager, was over fifty and never good himself at making jokes, even the old-fashioned kind. What was this word that everyone was using—'sophisticated'? The audiences were too sophisticated, even the children were: they seemed to have seen and heard all this before, even when they were too young to have seen and heard it.

'What shall we do?' he asked his wife. They were standing under the Big Top, which had just been put up, and wondering how many of the empty seats would still be empty when they gave their first performance. 'We shall have to do something, or it's a bad look-out.'

'I don't see what we can do about the comic side,' she said. 'It may come right by itself. Fashions change, all sorts of old things have returned to favour, like old-time dances. But there's something we could do.'

'What's that?'

'Put on an act that's dangerous, really dangerous. Audiences are never bored by that. I know you don't like it, and no more do I, but when we had the Wall of Death——'

Her husband's big chest-muscles twitched under his thin shirt.

'You know what happened then.'

'Yes, but it wasn't our fault, we were in the clear.'

He shook his head.

'Those things upset everyone. I know the public came after it happened—they came in shoals, they came to see the place where someone had been killed. But our people got the needle and didn't give a good performance for I don't know how long. If you're proposing another Wall of Death I wouldn't stand for it—besides, where will you find a man to do it?—especially with a lion on his bike, which is the great attraction.'

'But other turns are dangerous too, as well as dangerous-looking. It's *being* dangerous that is the draw.'

'Then what do you suggest?'

Before she had time to answer a man came up to them.

'I hope I don't butt in,' he said, 'but there's a man outside who wants to speak to you.'

'What about?'

'I think he's looking for a job.'

'Bring him in,' said the manager.

The man appeared, led by his escort, who then went away. He was a tall, sandy-haired fellow with tawny leonine eyes and a straggling moustache. It wasn't easy to tell his age—he might have been about thirty-five. He pulled off his old brown corduroy cap and waited.

'I hear you want to take a job with us,' the manager said, while his wife tried to size up the newcomer. 'We're pretty full up, you know. We don't take on strangers as a rule. Have you any references?'

'No, sir.'

'Then I'm afraid we can't help you. But just for form's sake, what can you do?'

As if measuring its height the man cast up his eyes to the point where one of the two poles of the Big Top was embedded in the canvas.

'I can dive sixty feet into a tank eight foot long by four foot wide by four foot deep.'

The manager stared at him.

'Can you now?' he said. 'If so, you're the very man we want. Are you prepared to let us see you do it?'

'Yes,' the man said.

'And would you do it with petrol burning on the water?'

'Yes.'

'But have we got a tank?' the manager's wife asked.

'There's the old Mermaid's tank. It's just the thing. Get somebody to fetch it.'

While the tank was being brought the stranger looked about him.

'Thinking better of it?' said the manager.

'No, sir,' the man replied. 'I was thinking I should want some bathing-trunks.'

'We can soon fix you up with those,' the manager said. 'I'll show you where to change.'

Leaving the stranger somewhere out of sight, he came back to his wife.

'Do you think we ought to let him do it?' she asked.

'Well, it's his funeral. You wanted us to have a dangerous act, and now we've got it.'

'Yes, I know, but——' The rest was drowned by the rattle of the trolley bringing in the tank—a hollow, double cube like a sarcophagus. Mermaids in low relief sported on its leaden flanks. Grunting and muttering to each other the men slid it into position, a few feet from the pole. Then a length of hose-pipe was fastened to a faucet, and soon they heard the sound of water swishing and gurgling in the tank.

'He's a long time changing,' said the manager's wife.

'Perhaps he's looking for a place to hide his money,' laughed her husband, and added, 'I think we'll give the petrol a miss.'

At length the man emerged from behind a screen, and slowly walked towards them. How tall he was, lanky and muscular. The hair on his body stuck out as if it had been combed. Hands on hips he stood beside them, his skin pimpled by goose-flesh. A fit of yawning overtook him.

'How do I get up?' he asked.

The manager was surprised, and pointed to the ladder. 'Unless you'd rather climb up, or be hauled up! You'll find a platform just below the top, to give you foot-hold.'

He had started to go up the chromium-plated ladder when the manager's wife called after him: 'Are you still sure you want to do it?'

'Quite sure, madam.'

He was too tall to stand upright on the platform, the awning brushed his head. Crouching and swaying forty feet above them he swung his arms as though to test the air's resistance. Then he pitched forward into space, unseen by the manager's wife who looked the other way until she heard a splash and saw a thin sheet of bright water shooting up.

The man was standing breast-high in the tank. He swung himself over the edge and crossed the ring towards them, his body dripping, his wet feet caked with sawdust, his tawny eyes a little bloodshot.

'Bravo!' said the manager, taking his shiny hand. 'It's a first-rate act, that, and will put money in our pockets. What do you want for it, fifteen quid a week?'

The man shook his head. The water trickled from his matted hair on to his shoulders, oozed from his borrowed bathing-suit and made runnels down his sinewy thighs. A fine figure of a man: the women would like him.

'Well, twenty then.'

Still the man shook his head.

'Let's make it twenty-five. That's the most we give any-one.'

Except for the slow shaking of his head the man might not have heard. The circus-manager and his wife exchanged a rapid glance.

'Look here,' he said. 'Taking into account the draw your act is likely to be, we're going to make you a special offer—thirty pounds a week. All right?'

Had the man understood? He put his finger in his mouth and went on shaking his head slowly, more to himself than at them, and seemingly unconscious of the bargain that was being held out to him. When he still didn't answer, the knot of tension broke, and the manager said, in his ordinary, brisk voice:

'Then I'm afraid we can't do business. But just as a matter of interest, tell us why you turned down our excellent offer.'

The man drew a long breath and breaking his long silence said, 'It's the first time I done it and I didn't like it.'

With that he turned on his heel and straddling his long legs walked off unsteadily in the direction of the dressing-room.

The circus-manager and his wife stared at each other.

'It was the first time he'd done it,' she muttered. 'The first time.' Not knowing what to say to him, whether to praise, blame, scold or sympathize, they waited for him to come back, but he didn't come.

'I'll go and see if he's all right,' the circus-manager said. But in two minutes he was back again. 'He's not there,' he said. 'He must have slipped out the other way, the crack-brained fellow!'

From *Two for the River* Copyright © L. P. Hartley.

Doris Lessing

DORIS LESSING, still a young writer, was born in Persia where her father at that time was working for the Imperial Bank of Persia. When she was five years old her family moved to Southern Rhodesia to farm maize. She spent most of her childhood on the farm and was educated at a convent and High School. She came to England in 1949 where she has been ever since.

When she came, she brought with her the manuscript of her first novel, *The Grass is Singing*, which was at once accepted, and reprinted six times. Since then, almost every year has seen a new book by Doris Lessing. Most of these have been collections of short stories. One collection, entitled *Five*, won the Somerset Maugham award in 1954 for the best literary work of the year by a British author under thirty-five.

Miss Lessing is also the author of a successful play, *Each His Own Wilderness*.

THROUGH THE TUNNEL

GOING TO the shore on the first morning of the holiday, the young English boy stopped at a turning of the path and looked down at a wild and rocky bay, and then over to the crowded beach he knew so well from other years. His mother walked on in front of him, carrying a bright-striped bag in one hand. Her other arm, swinging loose, was very white in the sun. The boy watched that white, naked arm, and turned his eyes, which had a frown behind them, toward the bay and back again to his mother. When she felt he was not with her, she swung around. 'Oh, there you are, Jerry!' she said. She looked impatient, then smiled. 'Why, darling, would you rather not come with me? Would you rather——' She frowned, conscientiously worrying over what amusements he might secretly be longing for which she had been too busy or too careless to imagine. He was very familiar with that anxious, apologetic smile. Contrition sent him running after her. And yet, as he ran, he looked back over his shoulder at the wild bay; and all morning, as he played on the safe beach, he was thinking of it.

Next morning, when it was time for the routine of swimming and sunbathing, his mother said, 'Are you tired of the usual beach, Jerry? Would you like to go somewhere else?'

'Oh, no!' he said quickly, smiling at her out of that unfailing impulse of contrition—a sort of chivalry. Yet, walking down the path with her, he blurted out, 'I'd like to go and have a look at those rocks down there.'

She gave the idea her attention. It was a wild-looking place, and there was no one there, but she said, 'Of course, Jerry. When you've had enough, come to the big beach. Or just go straight back to the villa, if you like.' She walked away, that bare arm, now slightly reddened from yesterday's sun, swinging. And he almost ran after her again, feeling it unbearable that she should go by herself, but he did not.

She was thinking, of course he's old enough to be safe without me. Have I been keeping him too close? He mustn't feel he ought to be with me. I must be careful.

He was an only child, eleven years old. She was a widow. She was determined to be neither possessive nor lacking in devotion. She went worrying off to her beach.

As for Jerry, once he saw that his mother had gained her beach, he began the steep descent to the bay. From where he was, high up among red-brown rocks, it was a scoop of moving bluish green fringed with white. As he went lower, he saw that it spread among small promontories and inlets of rough, sharp rock, and the crisping, lapping surface showed stains of purple and darker blue. Finally, as he ran sliding and scraping

6

down the last few yards, he saw an edge of white surf, and the shallow, luminous movement of water over white sand, and, beyond that, a solid, heavy blue.

He ran straight into the water and began swimming. He was a good swimmer. He went out fast over the gleaming sand, over a middle region where rocks lay like discoloured monsters under the surface, and then he was in the real sea—a warm sea where irregular cold currents from the deep water shocked his limbs.

When he was so far out that he could look back not only on the little bay but past the promontory that was between it and the big beach, he floated on the buoyant surface and looked for his mother. There she was, a speck of yellow under an umbrella that looked like a slice of orange peel. He swam back to shore, relieved at being sure she was there, but all at once very lonely.

On the edge of a small cape that marked the side of the bay away from the promontory was a loose scatter of rocks. Above them, some boys were stripping off their clothes. They came running, naked, down to the rocks. The English boy swam towards them, and kept his distance at a stone's throw. They were of that coast, all of them burned smooth dark brown, and speaking a language he did not understand. To be with them, of them, was a craving that filled his whole body. He swam a little closer; they turned and watched him with narrowed, alert dark eyes. Then one smiled and waved. It was enough. In a minute, he had swum in and was on the rocks beside them, smiling with a desperate, nervous supplication. They shouted cheerful greetings at him, and then, as he pre-served his nervous, uncomprehending smile, they understood that he was a foreigner strayed from his own beach, and they proceeded to forget him. But he was happy. He was with them.

They began diving again and again from a high point into a well of blue sea between rough, pointed rocks. After they had dived and come up, they swam around, hauled themselves up, and waited their turn to dive again. They were big boys—men to Jerry. He dived, and they watched him, and when he swam around to take his place, they made way for him. He felt he was accepted, and he dived again, carefully, proud of himself.

Soon the biggest of the boys poised himself, shot down into the water, and did not come up. The others stood about, watching. Jerry, after waiting for the sleek brown head to appear, let out a yell of warning; they looked at him idly and turned their eyes back towards the water. After a long time, the boy came up on the other side of a big dark rock, letting the air out of his lungs in a sputtering gasp and a shout of triumph. Immediately, the rest of them dived in. One moment, the morning seemed full of chattering boys; the next, the air and the surface of the water were empty. But through the heavy blue, dark shapes could be seen moving and groping.

Jerry dived, shot past the school of underwater swimmers, saw a black wall of rock looming at him, touched it, and bobbed up at once to the surface, where the wall was a low barrier he could see across. There was no one visible; under him, in the water, the dim shapes of the swimmers had disappeared. Then one, and then another of the boys came up on the far side of the barrier of rock, and he understood that they had swum through some gap or hole in it. He plunged down again. He could see nothing through the stinging salt water but the blank rock. When he came up, the boys were all on the diving rock, preparing to attempt the feat again. And now, in a panic of failure, he yelled up, in English, 'Look at me! Look!' And he began splashing and kicking in the water like a foolish dog.

They looked down gravely, frowning. He knew the frown. At moments of failure, when he clowned to claim his mother's attention, it was with just this grave, embarrassed inspection

that she rewarded him. Through his hot shame, feeling the
pleading grin on his face like a scar that he could never remove,
he looked up at the group of big brown boys on the rock and
shouted, '*Bonjour! Merci! Au revoir! Monsieur, monsieur!*' while
he hooked his fingers round his ears and waggled them.

Water surged into his mouth; he choked, sank, came up.
The rock, lately weighted with boys, seemed to rear up out of
the water as their weight was removed. They were flying down
past him, now, into the water; the air was full of falling bodies.
Then the rock was empty in the hot sunlight. He counted one,
two, three. . . .

At fifty, he was terrified. They must all be drowning beneath
him, in the watery caves of the rock! At a hundred, he stared
around him at the empty hillside, wondering if he should yell
for help. He counted faster, faster, to hurry them up, to bring
them to the surface quickly, to drown them quickly—anything
rather than the terror of counting on and on into the blue
emptiness of the morning. And then, at a hundred and sixty,
the water beyond the rock was full of boys blowing like brown
whales. They swam back to the shore without a look at him.

He climbed back to the diving rock and sat down, feeling
the hot roughness of it under his thighs. The boys were gathering up their bits of clothing and running off along the shore to
another promontory. They were leaving to get away from
him. He cried openly, fists in his eyes. There was no one to see
him, and he cried himself out.

It seemed to him that a long time had passed, and he swam
out to where he could see his mother. Yes, she was still there,
a yellow spot under an orange umbrella, he swam back to the
big rock, climbed up, and dived into the blue pool among the
fanged and angry boulders. Down he went, until he touched
the wall of rock again. But the salt was so painful in his eyes
that he could not see.

He came to the surface, swam to shore and went back to the villa to wait for his mother. Soon she walked slowly up the path, swinging her striped bag, the flushed, naked arm dangling beside her. 'I want some swimming goggles,' he panted, defiant and beseeching.

She gave him a patient, inquisitive look as she said casually, 'Well, of course, darling.'

But now, now, now! He must have them this minute, and no other time. He nagged and pestered until she went with him to a shop. As soon as she had bought the goggles, he grabbed them from her hand as if she were going to claim them for herself, and was off, running down the steep path to the bay.

Jerry swam out to the big barrier rock, adjusted the goggles, and dived. The impact of the water broke the rubber-enclosed vacuum, and the goggles came loose. He understood that he must swim down to the base of the rock from the surface of the water. He fixed the goggles tight and firm, filled his lungs, and floated, face down, on the water. Now he could see. It was as if he had eyes of a different kind—fish-eyes that showed everything clear and delicate and wavering in the bright water.

Under him, six or seven feet down, was a floor of perfectly clean, shining white sand, rippled firm and hard by the tides. Two greyish shapes steered there, like long, rounded pieces of wood or slate. They were fish. He saw them nose towards each other, poise motionless, make a dart forward, swerve off, and come around again. It was like a water dance. A few inches above them, the water sparkled as if sequins were dropping through it. Fish again—myriads of minute fish, the length of his fingernail, were drifting through the water, and in a moment he could feel the innumerable tiny touches of them against his limbs. It was like swimming in flaked silver. The great rock the big boys had swum through rose sheer out

of the white sand, black, tufted lightly with greenish weed.
He could see no gap in it. He swam down to its base.

Again and again he rose, took a big chestful of air, and went
down. Again and again he groped over the surface of the rock,
feeling it, almost hugging it in the desperate need to find the
entrance. And then, once, while he was clinging to the black
wall, his knees came up and he shot his feet out forward and
they met no obstacle. He had found the hole

He gained the surface, clambered about the stones that littered the barrier rock until he found a big one, and, with this
in his arms, let himself down over the side of the rock. He
dropped, with the weight, straight to the sandy floor. Clinging
tight to the anchor of stone, he lay on his side and looked in
under the dark shelf at the place where his feet had gone. He
could see the hole. It was an irregular, dark gap, but he could
not see deep into it. He let go of his anchor, clung with his
hands to the edges of the hole, and tried to push himself in.

He got his head in, found his shoulders jammed, moved
them in sidewise, and was inside as far as his waist. He could
see nothing ahead. Something soft and clammy touched his
mouth, he saw a dark frond moving against the greyish rock,
and panic filled him. He thought of octopuses, of clinging
weed. He pushed himself out backward and caught a glimpse,
as he retreated, of a harmless tentacle of seaweed drifting in the
mouth of the tunnel. But it was enough. He reached the sunlight, swam to shore, and lay on the diving rock. He looked
down into the blue well of water. He knew he must find his
way through that cave, or hole, or tunnel, and out the other
side.

First, he thought, he must learn to control his breathing. He
let himself down into the water with another big stone in his
arms, so that he could lie effortlessly on the bottom of the sea.
He counted. One, two, three. He counted steadily He could

hear the movement of blood in his chest. Fifty-one, fifty-two. . . . His chest was hurting. He let go of the rock and went up into the air. He saw that the sun was low. He rushed to the villa and found his mother at her supper. She said only, 'Did you enjoy yourself?' and he said, 'Yes.'

All night, the boy dreamed of the water-filled cave in the rock, and as soon as breakfast was over he went to the bay.

That night, his nose bled badly. For hours he had been underwater, learning to hold his breath, and now he felt weak and dizzy. His mother said, 'I shouldn't overdo things, darling, if I were you.'

That day and the next, Jerry exercised his lungs as if everything, the whole of his life, all that he would become, depended upon it. And again his nose bled at night, and his mother insisted on his coming with her the next day. It was a torment to him to waste a day of his careful self-training, but he stayed with her on that other beach, which now seemed a place for small children, a place where his mother might lie safe in the sun. It was not his beach.

He did not ask for permission, on the following day, to go to his beach. He went, before his mother could consider the complicated rights and wrongs of the matter. A day's rest, he discovered, had improved his count by ten. The big boys had made the passage while he counted a hundred and sixty. He had been counting fast, in his fright. Probably now, if he tried, he could get through that long tunnel, but he was not going to try yet. A curious, most unchildlike persistence, a controlled impatience, made him wait. In the meantime, he lay underwater on the white sand, littered now by stones he had brought down from the upper air, and studied the entrance to the tunnel. He knew every jut and corner of it, as far as it was possible to see. It was as if he already felt its sharpness about his shoulders.

He sat by the clock in the villa, when his mother was not

near, and checked his time. He was incredulous and then proud
to find he could hold his breath without strain for two minutes.
The words 'two minutes', authorized by the clock, brought the
adventure that was so necessary to him close.

In another four days, his mother said casually one morning,
they must go home. On the day before they left, he would do
it. He would do it if it killed him, he said defiantly to himself.
But two days before they were to leave—a day of triumph
when he increased his count by fifteen—his nose bled so badly
that he turned dizzy and had to lie limply over the big rock
like a bit of seaweed, watching the thick red blood flow on to
the rock and trickle slowly down to the sea. He was frightened.
Supposing he turned dizzy in the tunnel? Supposing he died
there, trapped? Supposing—his head went around, in the hot
sun, and he almost gave up. He thought he would return to
the house and lie down, and next summer, perhaps, when he
had another year's growth in him—*then* he would go through
the hole.

But even after he had made the decision, or thought he had,
he found himself sitting up on the rock and looking down into
the water, and he knew that now, this moment, when his nose
had only just stopped bleeding, when his head was still sore
and throbbing—this was the moment when he would try.
If he did not do it now, he never would. He was trembling with
fear that would not go, and he was trembling with horror at
that long, long tunnel under the rock, under the sea. Even in
the open sunlight, the barrier rock seemed very wide and very
heavy; tons of rock pressed down on where he would go. If he
died there, he would lie until one day—perhaps not before
next year—those big boys would swim into it and find it
blocked.

He put on his goggles, fitted them tight, tested the vacuum.
His hands were shaking. Then he chose the biggest stone he

could carry and slipped over the edge of the rock until half of him was in the cool, enclosing water and half in the hot sun. He looked up once at the empty sky, filled his lungs once, twice, and then sank fast to the bottom with the stone. He let it go and began to count. He took the edges of the hole in his hands and drew himself into it, wriggling his shoulders in sidewise as he remembered he must, kicking himself along with his feet.

Soon he was clear inside. He was in a small rock-bound hole filled with yellowish-grey water. The water was pushing him up against the roof. The roof was sharp and pained his back. He pulled himself along with his hands—fast, fast—and used his legs as levers. His head knocked against something; a sharp pain dizzied him. Fifty, fifty-one, fifty-two. . . . He was without light, and the water seemed to press upon him with the weight of rock. Seventy-one, seventy-two. . . . There was no strain on his lungs. He felt like an inflated balloon, his lungs were so light and easy, but his head was pulsing.

He was being continually pressed against the sharp roof, which felt slimy as well as sharp. Again he thought of octopuses, and wondered if the tunnel might be filled with weed that could tangle him. He gave himself a panicky, convulsive kick forward, ducked his head, and swam. His feet and hands moved freely, as if in open water. The hole must have widened out. He thought he must be swimming fast, and he was frightened of banging his head if the tunnel narrowed.

A hundred, a hundred and one. . . . The water paled. Victory filled him. His lungs were beginning to hurt. A few more strokes and he would be out. He was counting wildly; he said a hundred and fifteen, and then, a long time later, a hundred and fifteen again. The water was a clear jewel-green all around him. Then he saw, above his head, a crack running up through the rock. Sunlight was falling through it, showing the clean dark rock of the tunnel, a single mussel shell, and darkness ahead.

He was at the end of what he could do. He looked up at the crack as if it were filled with air and not water, as if he could put his mouth to it to draw air. A hundred and fifteen, he heard himself say inside his head—but he had said that long ago. He must go on into the blackness ahead, or he would drown. His head was swelling, his lungs cracking. A hundred and fifteen, a hundred and fifteen pounded through his head, and he feebly clutched at rocks in the dark, pulling himself forward, leaving the brief space of sunlit water behind. He felt he was dying. He was no longer quite conscious. He struggled on in the darkness between lapses into unconsciousness. An immense, swelling pain filled his head, and then the darkness cracked with an explosion of green light. His hands, groping forward, met nothing, and his feet, kicking back, propelled him out into the open sea.

He drifted to the surface, his face turned up to the air. He was gasping like a fish. He felt he would sink now and drown; he could not swim the few feet back to the rock. Then he was clutching it and pulling himself up on to it. He lay face down, gasping. He could see nothing but a red-veined, clotted dark. His eyes must have burst, he thought; they were full of blood. He tore off his goggles and a gout of blood went into the sea. His nose was bleeding, and the blood had filled the goggles.

He scooped up handfuls of water from the cool, salty sea, to splash on his face, and did not know whether it was blood or salt water he tasted. After a time, his heart quieted, his eyes cleared, and he sat up. He could see the local boys diving and playing half a mile away. He did not want them. He wanted nothing but to get back home and lie down.

In a short while, Jerry swam to shore and climbed slowly up the path to the villa. He flung himself on his bed and slept, waking at the sound of feet on the path outside. His mother was coming back. He rushed to the bathroom, thinking she must not see his face with bloodstains, or tearstains, on it. He came out of the bathroom and met her as she walked into the villa, smiling, her eyes lighting up.

'Have a nice morning?' she asked, laying her hand on his warm brown shoulder a moment.

'Oh, yes, thank you,' he said.

'You look a bit pale.' And then, sharp and anxious, 'How did you bang your head?'

'Oh, just banged it,' he told her.

She looked at him closely. He was strained, his eyes were glazed-looking. She was worried. And then she said to herself, 'Oh, don't fuss! Nothing can happen. He can swim like a fish.'

They sat down to lunch together.

'Mummy,' he said, 'I can stay under water for two minutes —three minutes, at least.' It came bursting out of him.

'Can you, darling?' she said. 'Well, I shouldn't overdo it. I don't think you ought to swim any more today.'

She was ready for a battle of wills, but he gave in at once. It was no longer of the least importance to go to the bay.

Isaac Asimov

ISAAC ASIMOV is a man of many talents. He is a Professor of Bio-chemistry at Boston University School of Medicine where he teaches, writes text books, and does research work on nucleic acids.

He is also a very successful writer of science-fiction, and of books for children. When his new house in Massachussets was being decorated the workmen stared at his choice of wallpaper for his study-cum-workroom. One of them, taking Mrs. Asimov aside, whispered, 'But doesn't the doctor realize that this is *children's* wall-paper?' Mrs. Asimov smiled.

The paper, patterned with pictures of planets and spaceships, was intended to serve as an inspiration for his books for young people.

THE FEELING OF POWER

JEHAN SHUMAN was used to dealing with the men in authority on long-embattled Earth. He was only a civilian but he originated programming patterns that resulted in self-directing war computers of the highest sort. Generals consequently listened to him. Heads of congressional committees, too.

There was one of each in the special lounge of New Pentagon. General Weider was space-burnt and had a small mouth puckered almost into a cipher. Congressman Brant was smooth-cheeked and clear-eyed. He smoked Denebian tobacco with the air of one whose patriotism was so notorious, he could be allowed such liberties.

Shuman, tall, distinguished, and Programmer-first-class, faced them fearlessly.

He said, 'Gentlemen, this is Myron Aub.'

'The one with the unusual gift that you discovered quite by

accident,' said Congressman Brant placidly. 'Ah.' He inspected the little man with the egg-bald head with amiable curiosity.

The little man, in return, twisted the fingers of his hands anxiously. He had never been near such great men before. He was only an ageing low-grade Technician who had long ago failed all tests designed to smoke out the gifted ones among mankind and had settled into the rut of unskilled labour. There was just this hobby of his that the great Programmer had found out about and was now making such a frightening fuss over.

General Weider said, 'I find this atmosphere of mystery childish.'

'You won't in a moment,' said Shuman. 'This is not something we can leak to the firstcomer.—Aub!' There was something imperative about his manner of biting off that one-syllable name, but then he was a great Programmer speaking to a mere Technician. 'Aub! How much is nine times seven?'

Aub hesitated a moment. His pale eyes glimmered with a feeble anxiety. 'Sixty-three,' he said.

Congressman Brant lifted his eyebrows. 'Is that right?'

'Check it for yourself, Congressman.'

The congressman took out his pocket computer, nudged the milled edges twice, looked at its face as it lay there in the palm of his hand, and put it back. He said, 'Is this the gift you brought us here to demonstrate. An illusionist?'

'More than that, sir. Aub has memorized a few operations and with them he computes on paper.'

'A paper computer?' said the general. He looked pained.

'No, sir,' said Shuman patiently. 'Not a paper computer. Simply a sheet of paper. General, would you be so kind as to suggest a number.'

'Seventeen,' said the general.

'And you, Congressman?'

'Twenty-three.'

'Good! Aub, multiply those numbers and please show the gentlemen your manner of doing it.'

'Yes, Programmer,' said Aub, ducking his head. He fished a small pad out of one shirt pocket and an artist's hairline stylus out of the other. His forehead corrugated as he made pains-taking marks on the paper.

General Weider interrupted him sharply. 'Let's see that.'

Aub passed him the paper, and Weider said, 'Well, it looks like the figure seventeen.'

Congressman Brant nodded and said, 'So it does, but I sup-pose anyone can copy figures off a computer. I think I could make a passable seventeen myself, even without practice.'

'If you will let Aub continue, gentlemen,' said Shuman without heat.

Aub continued, his hand trembling a little. Finally he said in a low voice, 'The answer is three hundred and ninety-one.'

Congressman Brant took out his computer a second time and flicked it, 'By Godfrey, so it is. How did he guess?'

'No guess, Congressman,' said Shuman. 'He computed that result. He did it on this sheet of paper.'

'Humbug,' said the general impatiently. 'A computer is one thing and marks on paper are another.'

'Explain, Aub,' said Shuman.

'Yes, Programmer—Well, gentlemen, I write down seven-teen and just underneath it I write twenty-three. Next I say to myself: seven times three——'

The congressman interrupted smoothly, 'Now, Aub, the problem is seventeen times twenty-three.'

'Yes, I know,' said the little Technician earnestly, 'but I *start* by saying seven times three because that's the way it works. Now seven times three is twenty-one.'

'And how do you know what?' asked the congressman.

'I just remember it. It's always twenty-one on the computer. I've checked it any number of times.'

'That doesn't mean that it always will be though, does it?' said the congressman.

'Maybe not,' stammered Aub. 'I'm not a mathematician. But I always get the right answers, you see.'

'Go on.'

'Seven times three is twenty-one, so I write down twenty-one. Then one times three is three, so I write down a three under the two of twenty-one.'

'Why under the two?' asked Congressman Brant at once.

'Because——' Aub looked helplessly at his superior for support. 'It's difficult to explain.'

Shuman said, 'If you will accept his work for the moment, we can leave the details for the mathematicians.'

Brant subsided.

Aub said, 'Three plus two makes five, you see, so the twenty-one becomes a fifty-one. Now you let that go for a while and start fresh. You multiply seven and two, that's fourteen, and one and two, that's two. Put them down like this and it adds up to thirty-four. Now if you put the thirty-four under the fifty-one this way and add them, you get three hundred and ninety-one and that's the answer.'

There was an instant's silence and then General Weider said, 'I don't believe it. He goes through this rigmarole and makes up numbers and multiplies and adds them this way and that, but I don't believe it. It's too complicated to be anything but horn-swoggling.'

'Oh no, sir,' said Aub in a sweat. 'It only *seems* complicated because you're not used to it. Actually, the rules are quite simple and will work for any numbers.'

'Any numbers, eh?' said the general. 'Come then.' He took

out his own computer (a severely styled GI model) and struck
it at random. 'Make a five seven three eight on the paper.
That's five thousand seven hundred and thirty-eight.'

'Yes, sir,' said Aub, taking a new sheet of paper.

'Now,' (more punching of his computer), 'seven two three
nine. Seven thousand two hundred and thirty-nine.'

'Yes, sir.'

'And now multiply those two.'

'It will take some time,' quavered Aub.

'Take the time,' said the general.

'Go ahead, Aub,' said Shuman crisply.

Aub set to work, bending low. He took another sheet of
paper and another. The general took out his watch finally and
stared at it. 'Are you through with your magic-making,
Technician?'

'I'm almost done, sir—Here it is, sir. Forty-one million,
five hundred and thirty-seven thousand, three hundred and
eighty-two.' He showed the scrawled figures of the result.

General Weider smiled bitterly. He pushed the multiplication contact on his computer and let the numbers whirl to a
halt. And then he stared and said in a surprised squeak, 'Great
Galaxy, the fella's right.'

The President of the Terrestrial Federation had grown hag-
gard in office and, in private, he allowed a look of settled
melancholy to appear on his sensitive features. The Denebian
war, after its early start of vast movement and great popularity,
had trickled down into a sordid matter of manoeuvre and
countermanoeuvre, with discontent rising steadily on Earth.
Possibly it was rising on Deneb, too.

And now Congressman Brant, head of the important
Committee on Military Appropriations, was cheerfully and
smoothly spending his half-hour appointment spouting
nonsense.

'Computing without a computer,' said the president impatiently, 'is a contradiction in terms.'

'Computing,' said the congressman, 'is only a system for handling data. A machine might do it, or the human brain might. Let me give you an example.' And, using the new skills he had learned, he worked out sums and products until the president, despite himself, grew interested.

'Does this always work?'

'Every time, Mr. President. It is foolproof.'

'Is it hard to learn?'

'It took me a week to get the real hang of it. I think you would do better.'

'Well,' said the president, considering, 'it's an interesting parlour game, but what is the use of it?'

'What is the use of a new-born baby, Mr. President? At the moment there is no use, but don't you see that this points the way towards liberation from the machine. Consider, Mr. President,' the congressman rose and his deep voice automatically took on some of the cadences he used in public debate, 'that the Denebian war is a war of computer against computer. Their computers forge an impenetrable field of counter-missiles against our missiles, and ours forge one against theirs. If we advance the efficiency of our computers, so do they theirs, and for five years a precarious and profitless balance has existed.

'Now we have in our hands a method for going beyond the computer, leapfrogging it, passing through it. We will combine the mechanics of computation with human thought; we will have the equivalent of intelligent computers; billions of them. I can't predict what the consequences will be in detail but they will be incalculable. And if Deneb beats us to the punch, they may be unimaginably catastrophic.'

The president said, troubled, 'What would you have me do?'

'Put the power of the administration behind the establishment of a secret project on human computation. Call it Project Number, if you like. I can vouch for my committee, but I will need the administration behind me.'

'But how far can human computation go?'

'There is no limit. According to Programmer Shuman, who first introduced me to this discovery——'

'I've heard of Shuman, of course.'

'Yes. Well, Dr. Shuman tells me that in theory there is nothing the computer can do that the human mind cannot do. The computer merely takes a finite amount of data and performs a finite number of operations upon them. The human mind can duplicate the process.'

The president considered that. He said, 'If Shuman says this, I am inclined to believe him—in theory. But, in practice, how can anyone know how a computer works?'

Brant laughed genially. 'Well, Mr. President, I asked the same question. It seems that at one time computers were designed directly by human beings. Those were simple computers, of course, this being before the time of the rational use of computers to design more advanced computers had been established.'

'Yes, yes. Go on.'

'Technician Aub apparently had, as his hobby, the reconstruction of some of these ancient devices and in so doing he studied the details of their workings and found he could imitate them. The multiplication I just performed for you is an imitation of the workings of a computer.'

'Amazing!'

The congressman coughed gently, 'If I may make another point, Mr. President—The further we can develop this thing, the more we can divert our Federal effort from computer production and computer maintenance. As the human brain takes over, more of our energy can be directed into peacetime pursuits and the impingement of war on the ordinary man will be less. This will be most advantageous to the party in power, of course.'

'Ah,' said the president, 'I see your point. Well, sit down, Congressman, sit down. I want some time to think about this. But meanwhile, show me that multiplication trick again. Let's see if I can't catch the point of it.'

Programmer Shuman did not try to hurry matters. Loesser was conservative, very conservative, and liked to deal with computers as his father and grandfather had. Still, he controlled the West European computer combine, and if he could be persuaded to join Project Number in full enthusiasm, a great deal would be accomplished.

But Loesser was holding back. He said, 'I'm not sure I like the idea of relaxing our hold on computers. The human mind is a capricious thing. The computer will give the same answer to the same problem each time. What guarantee have we that the human mind will do the same thing?'

'The human mind, Computer Loesser, only manipulates facts. It doesn't matter whether the human mind or a machine does it. They are just tools.'

'Yes, yes. I've gone over your ingenious demonstration that the mind can duplicate the computer, but it seems to me a little in the air. I'll grant the theory but what reason have we for thinking that the theory can be converted to practice?'

'I think we have reason, sir. After all, computers have not always existed. The cave men with their triremes, stone axes, and railroads had no computers.'

'And possibly they did not compute.'

'You know better than that. Even the building of a railroad or a ziggurat called for some computing, and that must have been without computers as we know them.'

'Do you suggest they computed in the fashion you demonstrate?'

'Probably not. After all, this method—we call it "graphitics", by the way, from the old European word "grapho" meaning "to write"—is developed from the computers themselves so it cannot have antedated them. Still, the cave men must have had *some* method, eh?'

'Lost arts! If you're going to talk about lost arts——'

'No, no. I'm not a lost art enthusiast, though I don't say there may not be some. After all, man was eating grain before hydroponics, and if the primitives ate grain, they must have grown it in soil. What else could they have done?'

'I don't know, but I'll believe in soil-growing when I see someone grow grain in soil. And I'll believe in making fire by rubbing two pieces of flint together when I see that, too.'

Shuman grew placative. 'Well, let's stick to graphitics. It's just part of the process of etherealization. Transportation by means of bulky contrivances is giving way to direct mass transference. Communications devices become less massive and more efficient constantly. For that matter, compare your pocket computer with the massive jobs of a thousand years ago. Why not, then, the last step of doing away with computers altogether? Come, sir, Project Number is a going concern, progress is already headlong. But we want your help. If patriotism doesn't move you, consider the intellectual adventure involved.'

Loesser said sceptically, 'What progress? What can you do beyond multiplication? Can you integrate a transcendental function?'

'In time, sir. In time. In the last month I have learned to handle division. I can determine, and correctly, integral quotients and decimal quotients.

'Decimal quotients? To how many places?'

Programmer Shuman tried to keep his tone casual. 'Any number!'

Loesser's jaw dropped. 'Without a computer?'

'Set me a problem.'

'Divide twenty-seven by thirteen. Take it to six places.'

Five minutes later, Shuman said, 'Two point oh seven six nine two three.'

Loesser checked it. 'Well, now, that's amazing. Multiplication didn't impress me too much because it involved integers after all, and I thought trick manipulation might do it. But decimals——'

'And that is not all. There is a new development that is, so far, top secret and which strictly speaking, I ought not to mention. Still—We may have made a breakthrough on the square root front.'

'Square roots?'

'It involves some tricky points and we haven't licked the bugs yet, but Technician Aub, the man who invented the science and who has an amazing intuition in connection with it, maintains he has the problem almost solved. And he is only a Technician. A man like yourself, a trained and talented mathematician ought to have no difficulty.'

'Square roots,' muttered Loesser, attracted.

'Cube roots, too. Are you with us?'

Loesser's hand thrust out suddenly. 'Count me in.'

General Weider stumped his way back and forth at the head of the room and addressed his listeners after the fashion of a savage teacher facing a group of recalcitrant students. It made no difference to the general that they were the civilian scientists heading Project Number. The general was the over-all head, and he so considered himself at every waking moment.

He said, 'Now square roots are fine, I can't do them myself and I don't understand the methods, but they're fine. Still the

Project will not be sidetracked into what some of you call the fundamentals. You can play with graphitics any way you want to after the war is over, but right now we have specific and very practical problems to solve.'

In a far corner, Technician Aub listened with painful attention. He was no longer a Technician, of course, having been relieved of his duties and assigned to the project, with a fine-sounding title and good pay. But, of course, the social distinctions remained and the highly placed scientific leaders could never bring themselves to admit him to their ranks on a footing of equality. Nor, to do Aub justice, did he, himself, wish it. He was as uncomfortable with them as they with him.

The general was saying, 'Our goal is a simple one, gentlemen: the replacement of the computer. A ship that can navigate space without a computer on board can be constructed in one-fifth the time and at one-tenth the expense of a computer-laden ship. We could build fleets five times, ten times, as great as Deneb could if we could eliminate the computer.

'And I see something even beyond this. It may be fantastic now, a mere dream; but in the future I see a manned missile!'

There was an instant murmur from the audience.

The general drove on. 'At the present time, our chief bottleneck is the fact that missiles are limited in intelligence. The computer controlling them can only be so large, and for that reason they can meet the changing nature of anti-missile defences in an unsatisfactory way. Few missiles, if any, accomplish their goal and missile warfare is coming to a dead end; for the enemy, fortunately, as well as for ourselves.

'On the other hand, a missile with a man or two within, controlling flight by graphitics, would be lighter, more mobile, more intelligent. It would give us a lead that might well mean the margin of victory. Besides which, gentlemen, the exigencies of war compel us to remember one thing. A man is much more dispensable than a computer. Manned missiles could be launched in numbers and under circumstances that no good general would care to undertake as far as computer-directed missiles are concerned——'

He said much more but Technician Aub did not wait.

Technician Aub, in the privacy of his quarters, laboured long over the note he was leaving behind. It read finally as follows:

'When I began the study of what is now called graphitics, it was no more than a hobby. I saw no more in it than an interesting amusement, an exercise of mind.

'When Project Number began, I thought that others were wiser than I; that graphitics might be put to practical use as a benefit to mankind, to aid in the production of really practical mass-transference devices perhaps. But now I see it is to be used only for death and destruction.

'I cannot face the responsibility involved in having invented graphitics.'

He then deliberately turned the focus of a protein-depolarizer on himself and fell instantly and painlessly dead.

They stood over the grave of the little Technician while tribute was paid to the greatness of his discovery.

Programmer Shuman bowed his head along with the rest of them, but remained unmoved. The Technician had done his share and was no longer needed, after all. He might have started graphitics, but now that it had started, it would carry on by itself overwhelmingly, triumphantly, until manned missiles were possible, with who knew what else.

Nine times seven, thought Shuman with deep satisfaction, is sixty-three, and I don't need a computer to tell me so. The computer is in my own head.

And it was amazing the feeling of power that gave him.

Questions

QUESTIONS I

THE WHITE RABBIT CAPER

1 James Thurber's stories have been called 'cartoons in words'. Do you think that phrase is a good description of this story? Why?
2 Thurber has used some of the style and technique of the fairy-tale in writing this story. Pick out some of the phrases that give it the fairy-tale atmosphere.
3 Much of the humour of this story is in Thurber's use of language and his play on words. Pick out five or six sentences which illustrate this.
4 Write another Fred Fox story in this style where he investigates the case of the missing canary and nails down Pious Parrot the undertaker as the culprit.

THE OPEN WINDOW

1 How, in the opening paragraph, does the writer set the scene?
2 Why is the sentence 'One would think he had seen a ghost' (p. 14) so effective?
3 How does the writer suggest, without actually saying so, that Mrs. Sappleton was not greatly interested in Nuttel?
4 Of the two stories that the girl told, which do you think is the more imaginative? Give your reasons.

THE REAPERS

1 Find six or seven descriptive, intimate touches that help to make this story vivid and alive.
2 With which of the characters do your sympathies lie? Why is this?
3 How are the dramatic effects achieved in this story?
4 Pick out the different ways in which Gill is contrasted with Considine and Bodkin.

THE VERTICAL LADDER

1 Do you think that this is a good title for this story? Suggest an alternative title.

2 There are a number of contrasts in this story. Mention some of them.

3 Collect details which make you feel that you are reading, not a work of fiction, but an account of an actual experience.

4 Why did Flegg not explain at the beginning that he had no head for heights?

5 How has the writer built up the suspense and drama in this story?

A CONFESSION

THE DEFEAT

1 Describe Don Camillo's own particular approach to God. (Have you read *Noah* by André Obey?)

2 Select one or two instances that show that the antagonism between Don Camillo and Peppone is more friendly than bitter.

3 Mention four or five ways in which Don Camillo does not fit into the conventional image of a priest.

4 Is Don Camillo the sort of person whose company and friendship you would enjoy? Why is this?

5 Giovanni Guareschi originally wrote these stories as anti-Communist propaganda. What sort of image of Communists was he trying to plant in the minds of his readers? In what ways do you think his approach might be more effective than a bitter, frontal attack?

THE MISER

1 Collect a few examples of the Irish idiom.

2 What do you find appealing, or unpleasant, about Faxy's character?

3 Much of the humour of this story lies in the reaction of the

characters to their circumstances. Find four or five examples of this.

4 The ending of the story is both unexpected and humorous. Where does the humour lie?

TACTICAL EXERCISE

1 Do you think that the title 'Tactical Exercise' is well chosen for this story? Why?
2 This is a story that has a twist at the end. What is the twist?
3 Why do you think that John Verney hated his wife?
4 The author lets us see into the mind of John, but not of Elizabeth. Why do you think this is so?
5 At the end of the story do you think that John has really been drugged? Outline the events which might have immediately followed on from the end of this story.

HENRY

1 What was Fletcher's opinion of the lion-tamer? Why did he feel that lions were inferior beasts to his tigers? Which sentence expresses his contempt of the lions?
2 What is the significance of the line, 'A man does not kill his god; at least not willingly. Two thousand years ago he did some such thing, perhaps through ignorance; but Fletcher forgot this incident.'? Why do you think the writer introduced this reference to Christ?
3 Mention some of the chief differences between the characters of Fletcher and Macormack.
4 What do you learn from the story about the qualities needed by an animal trainer?

THE MAN WHO KNEW HOW

1 Did the ending of the story come as a surprise to you? If so, what did you expect it to be? If it was not a surprise, where in the story did you first realize what the outcome would be?
2 What picture do you form of Pender?

3 Why did Buckley's story seem so convincing?

4 How would you have tried to convince Pender that his suspicions of Buckley were unreasonable and absurd?

THE OLD MAN

1 This story is told in the first person. Does the story gain anything from this method of telling?

2 Now that you know the end of the story, are you aware of any details or incidents that should have made you suspect that the characters were other than human?

3 Which is most prominent in this story—plot, characterization, or setting? Write a few words on each.

4 Do you think the story would have gained anything if the identity of the swans had been revealed earlier in the story?

COMPASSION CIRCUIT

1 Find evidence in the extract to show that Janet was an extremely sensitive woman.

2 Do you find this story convincing? Give reasons for your answer.

3 What is there about this story that might be either horrifying, or amusing?

4 Why do you think that the writer has omitted to put into words the fate of George and Janet, but has inferred it only.

THE DIAMOND HAIR-PIN

1 What reasons do you suppose led Aimée Vibert to reply to the newspaper advertisement?

2 Dialogue can illustrate the characters of the speakers, help on the action, and liven up the story. Discuss the use made of dialogue in this story.

3 When, during the course of the story, did Tom Wakeling find himself in a dilemma? What did he do about it?

4 Write out the letter that you think Tom might have received from the elderly and acidly irate lady.

A HIGH DIVE

1 Where do you think the climax comes in this story?
2 In a short story the beginning and ending are very important. Would you call them especially effective in 'The High Dive'? Give your reasons.
3 Compare this story with 'The Open Window'. What similarities—and differences—do you notice?
4 Do you agree that dangerous acts will draw larger audiences? Why should this be so?
5 Good, natural dialogue is one of the hardest things to write. How far do you think that the author has succeeded in this story in writing good dialogue?

THROUGH THE TUNNEL

1 Do you think it important to the story that Jerry's mother was a widow?
2 Why did Jerry so desperately want to swim through the tunnel? Were his motives the same at the end of the story as at the beginning?
3 In many ways Jerry was most unchildlike. Find three or four examples which support this.
4 Miss Lessing's unsentimental presentation of scenes and people, her compassionate understanding, her eye for detail, and her power to convey atmosphere make this a moving story. Quote examples which illustrate these aspects of the author's skill.

THE FEELING OF POWER

1 By what internal evidence can you fix the approximate period in which this story is set?
2 What modern parallel can you find for the predicament that faced Technician Aub at the end of the story? Can you find any other problems and attitudes of the present day that the author has included in this story?

3 What arguments does Congressman Brant use to persuade the President to back Project Number?

4 Where do you think the climax comes in this story?

5 In what way is this story different from most other stories which look into the future?

QUESTIONS II

1 The story-teller who is a master of his craft can, in the first few sentences, set the scene, introduce the main characters, and hint at the problems that the hero has to solve. Which story, in your opinion, has the best opening? Give your reasons.

2 Some writers of science-fiction present ideas which are quite credible, others seem far fetched. Into which category do you think the science-fiction stories in this book come? Give your reasons.

3 There is an old saying: 'By their deeds ye shall know them'. Some writers bring depth to their characters by showing them in action. Which story does this most effectively?

4 Mention two stories which depend for their effect on a surprise ending. How is this effected?

5 Which story have you found most amusing? Say why you found it so.

6 Choose the story which, in your opinion, would make a good film. Give reasons.

7 Mention one story which is remarkable for its atmosphere. How has the writer achieved it?

8 Write a short review suitable for a magazine, of one of the stories in this book.